STOLEN FIRE

STOLEN FIRE

NOAH SERIES
BOOK 2

JORDYN KROSS

Published by Scarlet Parlor Press, LLC

Library of Congress Control Number: 2025917684

Publisher's Cataloging-in-Publication

(Provided by Cassidy Cataloguing Services, Inc.)

Names: Kross, Jordyn, author.
Title: Stolen fire / Jordyn Kross.
Description: [Albuquerque, New Mexico] : Scarlet Parlor Press, LLC, [2025] | Series: Kross, Jordyn. NOAH series ; bk. 2.
Identifiers: LCCN: 2025917684 | ISBN: 9781959691174 (paperback) | 9781959691167 (ebook)
Subjects: LCSH: Extraterrestrial beings--Fiction. | Engineers--Fiction. | Shapeshifting--Fiction. | Space ships--Fiction. | Love--Fiction. | Carriers--Fiction. | LCGFT: Erotic fiction. | Romance fiction. | Science fiction. | BISAC: FICTION / Romance / Science Fiction. | FICTION / Romance / Erotic. | FICTION / Science Fiction / Space Opera.
Classification: LCC: PS3611.R776 S76 2025 | DDC: 813/.6--dc23

Editors: Dayna Hart

Jenny Rardon

Cover: Brandi Doane McCann

Find all of Jordyn's books at jordynkross.com or here:

Melting Hearts Series

Prequel Novella - Jack's Frost

(free for newsletter subscribers)

Book 1 - Winter's List

Book 2 - Xmas Angel

Book 3 - Shattered Ice

The Yacht Club Series

Book 1 - The Handler

Book 2 - The Wrangler

Dirty Daisy Mystery Series

Book 1 - Dirty Daisy

Book 2 - Hell Hath No Furry

Uhraervi Brothers

Hung with Care

Open Enrollment

Pole Position

Fool's Gold

NOAH Series

Prequel Novella - Quantum Entanglements

Book 1 - Captain's Treasure

Book 2 - Stolen Fire

Nonfiction

Demystifying the Beats

Author Survival Guide

Single Titles

A Lost Claus

Dedicated to all the smart ones who embraced their identity, adapted, and overcame.

CHAPTER 1

1017 A. N., Planet Kolben, at the far edge of the Gliese Solar System.

Furcifer "Cifer" Msuya had made many poor decisions in his life, but accepting the retrieval job from the Hiargus royal family might be his last.

If he had known what a clusterfuck the job would be, he'd have doubled his exorbitant quote. Across the snow-dusted launch deck, he tracked the path of Jarn, the man who'd promised that his captain would get Cifer off this ass-sucking iceberg of a planet. He'd already been stuck there far longer than he'd anticipated. It had been much easier to sneak onto the planet than to escape.

The tips of his fingers burned with pain, and he blew on them to warm them before checking on the package—the reason he'd come to Kolben. He didn't dare touch it again—he'd already been warned. It was bad enough having it tucked into a pouch against his body.

Jarn carried a large metal box and disappeared behind an enormous transport ship before reappearing—arms empty—

running full tilt toward the low administration buildings in the distance. Where was he going? Jarn had said to meet him. His captain would take Cifer wherever he wished to go. Cifer had paid the guy up front.

Barking dogs sprinted from the transport ship, followed by a huge bald man. They raced behind the vehicle that Jarn had come from. Cifer remained hidden in the depression at the edge of the launch deck, waiting to see what new catastrophe sparked.

The dogs and the big bald man reappeared. He carried the metallic case Jarn had left behind. The dogs halted in a pack, but the man kept running. He froze at the edge of the far field. With an athletic twist, he hurled the case, which exploded midair.

Cifer dropped down flat into the gully, no longer feeling the cold. His heart raced. Alarms screamed. He lifted his head. Vehicles raced to the blackened spot and across the platform in the opposite direction. A spaceship went hot, engines flaring. The other ship on the deck, the one on which Jarn had promised Cifer passage, lifted from the ground and disappeared into the sky.

What the fuck!

No.

That did *not* happen.

Not only was he out of credits in the one account he could access, but the mining company would be on high alert. They would have no problem detaining him for his probably very short life if it came to that. His other account would cover any emergencies for the orphanage, but not for long. Heavy dread weighed him deeper into the snow-filled gully.

Vehicles came and went. Several crew members had emerged from the large transport ship. The bald man and the dogs had been taken away. Jarn had been found and carted off in a different direction during the chaos. After what seemed like hours of lying in the snowbank, Cifer had to move. The risk of dying competed with the risk of being caught.

He slowly stood and gradually moved around the launch deck, finally reaching the far side of a huge hauler. His shifting shadow increased the risk of being noticed despite his camouflage. But a moment later, he blended into the gray surface of the ship. *The Treasure.*

How fitting a ship name for a thief to use for their getaway.

The front of the vehicle was the typical rounded bridge with space-proof viewing portals. Smaller portals ran equidistance down the side of the top edge. Must be the quarters, but that was an expensive feature. Someone had invested heavily in this transporter. The lower part of the ship and the back third were solid and larger than the bridge and quarters combined. There would be plenty of places to hide once he was onboard.

A ship this big could easily have a crew of fifty, but he'd only counted five—six with the bald man. Inside, there could be additional staff or, worse, more dogs.

The wide, unguarded loading bay invited him in, but "easy" often led to "caught." He inched nearer to his only chance for escape. Silence. He glanced at the empty sky. The urge to hunt Jarn's captain, who'd literally dropped a bomb and run off with Cifer's credits—but without Cifer himself—heated his blood. There would be retribution, but only once the time came. No need to rush. The first step on the gangplank made his skin tingle. Slow, deep breaths. No one could see him.

Once inside the utilitarian loading space, he noted two options: an elevator, and a ladder positioned at opposite ends of the cavernous room. Cifer crept toward the ladder, his movements as slow as he could make them, considering the urgency of his mission.

The ship remained quiet, and it was noticeably warmer.

That factor was enough to get him moving, inside and farther back, away from the bridge. In his experience, shipboard inhabitants tended to congregate in the activity centers, like galleys, bridges, and common rooms—places he would avoid.

Stowaways were dealt with in a variety of manners, none of which encouraged the practice.

He really was getting too old for life-or-death escapes. A quick pat of the sack slung under his cloak assured him that he was still in possession of the orb.

Yip!

Shit. The dogs. Cipher froze, in plain view of the opening to the large port-less part of the ship.

A high-pitched, needy whine came from a single pup in a large crate, wriggling around, dancing back and forth and lifting up onto...*her* back legs, begging for attention. If he didn't quiet the puppy, she'd expose him.

"Good girl," he whispered. Nothing else moved. There was a storage locker in front of the crate. Cifer lifted the lid, and the puppy bounced, chirping excitedly. Cifer retrieved a meat stick, and the pup immediately sat, eyes focused on him despite his camouflage. Anyone glancing in would see a treat floating in the air. Cifer brought his finger to his lips and slipped the treat through the holes of the wire mesh. The pup licked his fingers before taking the meat gently between her needle teeth and retreating to the back of the crate.

Cifer didn't waste time moving deeper into the ship, away from the cute, but potentially effective, alarm system. He sidled past larger locked cells and a few stout crates. A sizable room on his left held plants growing out of sacks. He backed away, deeper into the far areas of the ship, and found the engine room. Tubes and large mechanical equipment filled the room from edge to edge. Perfect. Despite the bright overhead lighting, infinite nooks and crannies would provide concealment and—once the engines fired up—warm his frozen body. He'd like to be reintroduced to his balls.

Voices floated back to the silent space where Cifer had curled up in who knew how long ago. There were sounds of machinery, men's voices, and the thunk of crates on a metal floor. He pressed himself into the shadows and prayed for luck. His large body couldn't lose mass, but he could shape it to fit where he needed.

Periodically, females came to check on the pup. He couldn't tell the voices apart. Only the pitch gave away the fact that the males had left the transport. He took no relief. Females could be vicious when defending themselves, especially in a pack. Trails of the scent of burned food traced back to him, killing his immediate hunger pains. In another cycle or two, he wouldn't care if the food was edible, but he wasn't desperate yet...except to get moving. The faster he got off Kolben, the faster he could deliver the orb and collect his fee.

Finally, the engines ignited. A voice, husky and sweet, rolled through the room. He fought the urge to leave his hiding spot and view the owner to see if she was as luscious as the tones promised. His stomach grumbled, arguing the first order of business was food. Thankfully, the sound didn't carry over the engines. And his stomach was wrong. First, get off the planet. Then food. Then find the hot female and— *No.*

Then deliver the orb before whatever supposed influence it possessed worked on him. The funds tied to the delivery would sustain him and his obligations for a long time. He could find the female later if he still cared to. *The Treasure* wouldn't be a hard ship to track down.

Any moment, the ship would lift off.

...

Any moment.

Cifer took a slow, deep breath, drawing on his well of patience, which was at an all-time low. The ship shuddered and lifted. *Yes.* They hovered, and Cifer braced for launch. Hold... Hold... The ship dropped back to the launchpad.

The engines shut down.

Fuck no.

They *had* to launch.

He had to go. Should have already gone. Insanity teased him—for a moment, he considered showing himself and demanding an explanation. He slowed his breathing. In a situation where he had no control, his only control was his response.

Slow in. Slow out.

Eventually, he leveled out. Not like the ship would remain on Kolben. It had to take off sometime, but damn, he really wished the ride with Jarn had worked out.

Pain in Cifer's gut woke him. He hadn't meant to fall asleep. Dangerous. But he hadn't slept or eaten well since he'd landed on Kolben. Once out of his hiding place, he hesitated. Nothing moved. The slow susurration of the basic mechanical systems filled the space. He crept out of the engine room, letting the shadows assist his natural cloaking. The puppy remained splayed on a cushion at the back of the crate, oblivious to Cifer's presence.

He reached the entrance ladder that led to the lower deck and froze, using all his senses. Nothing moved. No sounds. No scent of food. He crept down a large corridor packed with storage cabinets. A doorway on his right called to him. The faint scent of past meals made his mouth water. With no time to waste, he hurried to investigate and found protein bars. He took an entire row so the appearance at a casual glance would remain the same. Shoving one into his mouth and the rest into his cloaked pouch, he chewed quickly as he rushed on silent feet back to safety and his interminable wait.

Another cycle passed slowly. Cifer couldn't risk exploring. Every time he considered it, someone came to check on the dog or deliveries came. More crates. Fuels rods. Protein bars gone, Cifer entertained himself with searching for small, discarded items in the far reaches of the engine room. The room was surprisingly clean, which added to his boredom. A bolt had been the best find. But giving into the tediousness of the waiting—allowing himself to leave his spot—would be the death of him. One hand, feeling along the edges of boxes, under crates, seemed a reasonable compromise.

The air changed. He pulled his arm slowly back to his hiding spot.

"Captain, I was able to get more fuel rods. They've been loaded, and we should have enough to get to Cassan, even if we don't take the ER bridge, but I think Rhysa said we are taking the wormhole? Did you authorize that? I mean, it's good, but I need to do other checks for that kind of travel. Take additional precautions."

The voice was lush and intelligent, if a bit rushed. The same voice that had seduced him cycles earlier. If only he could poke his head out to put a face with the voice. The voices faded as they left the cargo area. Cifer took a step to follow. Sanity slapped him back into place. He'd waited this long and was so close to escaping. *Don't fuck it up.*

He slipped open the flap of his pouch. It was hard to believe that the rounded stone was so important to the royal family. He'd tripled his fees when they contacted him. A trip to Kolben wasn't something he'd ever wanted to do. The planet, owned by a mining company, held a horde of sentient beings working as slaves for the remainder of their attenuated lives. His brief glimpse into the workforce had left him unsettled. Beings aging before their time. If—*when*— he survived this job, he'd investigate just how they acquired their workers.

Cifer shivered and returned the swirling ball in its protective shroud. He wasn't off the planet yet. The cloth of the bag had cost him plenty, along with the clothes he wore. The expensive fabric was normally used for women's gowns in the more risqué circles. It took on the coloring of the wearer, through some kind of light scattering that he didn't entirely understand. All he knew was that he was warmer and still able to use his natural ability to camouflage. The cost would be justified when he collected the other part of his fee.

If he collected it.

Voices carried down the corridor, warning him of the crew members' approach. The sexy voice he'd heard earlier reached his ears, but the words were unclear. They weren't close enough. The female was a talker. Cifer laughed a little to himself. He would always know where she was on the ship.

"I need to check my plants. I had no idea Cyra would authorize an ER jump."

"I know. I'm not ready either." The enticing female had returned. He hadn't even seen her yet, and already the urge to possess her threaded through him. "We have to lock down everything. Thankfully, the fuel was delivered. Not that it was late—this was just the latest window—but I hate waiting. It would be so much easier if they just showed up on time, like at the earliest time they say, instead of having to wait and wonder if they are going to arrive and if you should contact them. But you don't want to get on their bad side, especially on a planet with only one supplier. That wouldn't do."

"Okay." The gentle voice interrupted the other female. "I'll check on my plants now. I'll see you later in the galley. I think we may have some peppers ready to harvest."

The room with the plants made more sense, but it was very unusual. Cifer pressed a hand to his stomach when it growled in anticipation. He'd nearly starved on Kolben. What organization keeps its food stores under lock and key?

"Are you hungry?"

The velvet tones coaxed him to answer. He opened his mouth.

"I have the fuel rods you need, hungry beast."

He clacked his jaw shut. Cifer wasn't sure which outcome he craved more: having her come closer so he could see her, or having her stay away so he wouldn't be discovered. He rolled his eyes at himself.

No female—nobody—was worth being discovered and ejected from the ship before they ever got into space. Before he ever delivered the sphere. Before he got the biggest payout for a heist he'd ever contracted.

CHAPTER 2

Blaize reached the galley last, again. Working in the farthest bowels of the ship and doing some seriously dirty jobs meant she had the farthest to travel and the most cleanup to do before she joined the rest of the crew. Did they even notice she wasn't present?

Rhysa and Bodi sat on opposite sides of the anchored metal table, not looking at each other. Despite the fact that Bodi was a communications specialist and Rhysa an expert navigator, those two couldn't find a way to talk without arguing. Veda, head down, focused on the table. Whatever Rhysa and Bodi had said before she arrived must have upset the kind medic. Captain Cyra chattered brightly to her lover and the security officer slash chef, Dez, about what he was making for dinner. Dez shouldn't be cooking. Probably shouldn't be out of bed after saving *The Treasure* from a bomb. But if Cyra was okay with it, who was she to comment?

"It smells really good, whatever it is." Blaize took a seat between Veda and Rhysa, leaving the seat next to Cyra for Dez. The table was long, and they each had plenty of space to spread out.

"Blaize," Dez said with a welcoming tone as he pulled the lid off the food he'd prepared on the induction plate. Cyra jumped up to help him. "Now that you're here, I can serve."

Someone *had* noted Blaize's absence.

"Sit, love," Dez said to Cyra, his voice almost too low to hear.

"You just got out of the hospital. Your hand." Cyra stared pointedly at Dez's arm, which ended in a stump.

He kissed the top of her head. Cyra picked up the plates as Dez loaded them, and she passed them around the table.

Blaize leaned over and nudged Veda with her shoulder. The medic popped up her head and gave her a small smile. "So, first harvest? Are you excited? I know I am. Of course, I'm so hungry I could probably eat anything, but this smells amazing. What did you get?"

Cyra placed a plate in front of Blaize.

"Oh wow. It looks really good." Blaize couldn't help staring at the real—not freeze-dried—peppers diced on top of what looked like a synth protein and ricex dish. She would do everything she could to stay on the ship that not only let her be the sole engineer but was supplied with fresh food.

"Eat." Dez lifted his fork and dug in.

Everyone else followed his example.

"Veda, congratulations." Cyra smiled warmly at her best friend. "When you told me what you were going to attempt gardening in space, I wasn't sure it would work. You've exceeded all expectations."

"Only tomatoes and peppers so far. But more will come." Veda spoke softly but with confidence. "I have some more prep to do before we leave, to make sure nothing is damaged during our jump."

"I've been reviewing the systems, and everything appears

ready from my end," Blaize said. "The fuel is high quality. As good as what we get on Cassan or possibly better—although for the price, it should be. Everything is so expensive here. But that's to be—"

"Speaking of expenses. Each of you has a share of the profit on this run coming to them," Cyra interrupted.

Blaize clamped her jaw shut. She talked too much.

"I do have enough to pay all of you back and cover the expenses of the return trip to Cassan."

Rhysa's pink eyes flashed almost red when she looked up. "Captain," she said sharply. "Are you telling us you don't want us as partners, only paid crew members?"

Bodi's small wings twitched. "That isn't what she said. If you'd let her finish, you wouldn't need to argue."

"Who's arguing now?" Rhysa snapped.

"Let me explain," Cyra spoke above them both. "Dez secured a contract to return some unneeded equipment to Cassan for pickup by the vendor. The mining operation has ongoing contracts for their mineral production deliveries and their supply orders, so we couldn't get any traction on that front. But they did have equipment that needed to go back, and no one has been able to take it for them. These are one-shot deals, but they will cover our return to Cassan with plenty left over. So, I can pay anyone out who doesn't want to stay. I hope all of you will elect to remain." She silently met each of their gazes for a moment.

Blaize blinked to break the connection, unfamiliar with such respect.

"If you want to remain a partner, great." Cyra smiled at Veda. "If you would prefer to be a paid crew member, that can be accommodated. I wanted to bring it up now so you have time to consider your decision. I'll need to know your plans when we get to Cassan."

"Will you be adding to the crew, and if so, will they be given the option to buy in as a partner?" Rhysa asked.

Blaize tensed. She hadn't considered that an option.

"I'm not opposed to adding to the crew. I know the engineering job is huge. But I'm not planning to recruit unless one of you makes a request for additional crew. If we find someone, all the active partners would have to decide if the person would be offered a partnership."

Blaize tried not to panic. Why had the captain mentioned engineering? Did Cyra think she wasn't doing her job? The ship was running at ninety-two percent efficiency. Anything over ninety was considered exceptional, but maybe Cyra only saw the room for improvement. Maybe she thought someone else could do a better job. And with the funds to buy Blaize out... Blaize choked down the rest of her meal.

"Before we make any decisions on how to split the profits, it's only right to cover the costs of Dez's injury." Veda paused to give each of them a pointed look. "He lost his hand saving the ship. Prosthetics—good ones, which integrate—are expensive."

"I'm not even sure that's possible, Veda." Dez smiled at the medic. "If it is, we can look into the costs and how to cover them at that point."

"She's right." Rhysa pointed at Veda with her fork, and Bodi nodded.

"I'm going to mechanical." Blaize stood and took her dishes to the sanitizer. "There are a few things I want to look over again."

"The final crate of equipment is supposed to be delivered first thing tomorrow. As soon as we're loaded and have authorization, we'll leave," Cyra said.

Blaize acknowledged the captain before rushing out of the galley so she wouldn't say anything she'd regret. Her steps echoed through the wide, well-lit hallways. The cabinets lining the corridor were a bit grimy from use. Above the ceiling and below the floor, various cables and conduits needed to connect all the ship's systems. Blaize felt more at home on *The Treasure* than she'd ever felt in the caverns of her home planet. If Cyra thought she wasn't doing an adequate job, she wouldn't be able to stay.

Veda was wonderful and warm, and it was nice to chat with her about the plants. Rhysa and Bodi, although they liked to snipe at each other, were fun, fascinating and, from what she could tell, honest. The other females on her planet had ostracized her for her mixed heritage and odd appearance. *The Treasure's* crew were the first female friends she'd ever had. She would do everything possible to remain. She walked a little faster, running through a mental list of tasks she could perform to make sure the trip through the ER bridge was as smooth as possible. That might earn her points with a captain who hated ER travel.

As Blaize passed the opening to the greenhouse, she caught a movement in her peripheral vision. She paused and entered the room, checking the ceiling and the floor. She crouched and peered under the tables. There was nothing there. It must have been a trick of her mind, but she would be more vigilant. It didn't seem likely that there would be vermin on an ice planet, but it was still possible. Gnawing rodents could spell huge trouble for the systems if they accessed the ship and went unchecked.

She stared back over her shoulder as she exited the room and almost ran over Veda.

"Blaize, I'm glad you're here." Veda gripped her arm. "I wanted to ask you if there is anything else I should do to get ready for the jump?"

Veda proceeded to show her how each plant was secured and the fine-mesh netting over the dirt. Blaize forced herself to focus on Veda, despite the eerie sense that she was being watched.

"We should check the shelves. Make sure they're anchored, along with the lights. When did you install them? Did Dez help you? I have a wrench in engineering. Give me a minute." Blaize raced to the cabinet where she stored her tools and retrieved her favorite wrench. It was probably overkill for the job but would help with the vulnerable sensation she couldn't shake.

"Wow. That's huge," Veda said when Blaize returned.

"That's what she said." Blaize couldn't help the stupid joke. The itchy feel of eyes on her had returned. "It's actually very useful since it's so long and adjustable. The leverage means I don't need as much physical strength to tighten the bolts. It's a little unwieldy overhead, but since you have these shelves spaced like ladders, I should be fine."

As soon as Blaize could, she left Veda and went deeper into the ship, where she had some control.

The systems did what you set them to do. The settings were either right or wrong. There was no ambiguity when it came to engineering. Systems were either working optimally, or they weren't. It was so much easier than dealing with people. Some days, she missed having her own ship, but then she remembered how much she hated managing a crew. And how much it hurt when they all abandoned her. Staying on with Cyra would be the best possible future. *If* she could get the captain to see she was capable of doing the job without adding engineering staff to second-guess every move Blaize made. Or worse, force her into the junior role.

A shadow caught her eye. Did something move? She crawled all over the systems, tugging the connections, and tightening every bolt, but couldn't find anything that wasn't latched down. No evidence of animals, but the odd sense of being watched continued. Paranoia hadn't plagued her so relentlessly since she'd been with Varik. Only he *had* been after her. She checked the time. Late. She could keep going, but a yawn had her heading to her quarters. She'd done what she could to prepare for the wormhole. It would have to be enough.

CHAPTER 3

"Where are you going, lover?" The hybrid escort lounged against the padded frame of the bunk, two of their three breasts exposed and still bearing some exquisite bite marks.

Varik couldn't help the grin that touched his lips. But no matter how entertaining the time on this fuck-all of an excuse for a station had been, it was time to go. According to the brief conversation he'd had with Karnek, the ship was ready with a whole new identity.

Varik slipped a leg into his coveralls. "Been fun."

"When will you be back?"

Never. Because if he had to come back, it meant his plans were falling apart. Again. "Soon. Behave while I'm gone, or I'll put your dick in a cock cage and beat your ass without mercy."

The hybrid—Varik couldn't remember their name—shivered and moaned. Never let it be said he left his sexual partners unsatisfied. Maybe a bit bitter, but always fully pleasured.

With a quick seal of his coveralls, he darted out the door and down the poorly lit underground tunnel. Occasionally, a scream, or something worse, emanated from the doors he passed. If he'd had time, he'd have stopped to see if they were open and if he could enjoy the spectacle of whatever was happening to make those thrilling sounds.

Karnek stood outside the ship. It shone, the paint of the new name, *Cain's Alibi*, without a single blemish from space dust or ER bridge crossings. So perfect, he ought to record an image. Varik rolled his eyes at himself. "Let's go."

Varik entered the security code into his comm and transmitted it to his vessel. The bay door lowered. "Did you get the fuel?"

"We're fully stocked. I did what I could to negotiate."

The likelihood of a successful negotiation on a 3F station—fuel, fix, fuck—was infinitesimally small. Varik pulled up the receipt and scowled, mainly for Karnek's benefit. "Where'd you learn to negotiate?"

Karnek sputtered.

Varik stomped up the ramp, grinning on the inside. Never a good idea to give many compliments. Leave your lessers grasping and desperate for approval.

"Run a scan as soon as we launch and clear the quiet zone. I want to know if *The Treasure* is anywhere nearby." And blast it out of space, but unfortunately, his ship wasn't designed for battle. It favored research and steady performance. There were modifications Varik would make to increase the speed, but it would never be fast, which made navigation even more important.

Varik strapped into the captain's seat, even though there would be no need to punch out of the atmosphere. Once the port doors opened, they could basically float out. Everything on the 3F was in an artificially created atmosphere, mostly underground. Ingenious way to stay beyond the reach of any judicial oversight from a nearby planet. Varik almost wished he'd thought of it first. With the prices they charged, they had to be making a fortune.

As soon as they were outside the quiet zone around the 3F, Varik reminded Karnek to initiate a deep search for *The Treasure*. They had to be out here somewhere. That bitch who stole his ship was too weak to use ER bridges. "I entered a course for the Cassan space station. You keep an eye on the search."

"Yes, sir."

"I'm going to get cleaned up, unless you can't handle the ship by yourself."

"No, sir, I'm fine. Glad you got us off Kolben when you did. I don't know what I would have done if we'd been stuck there. And thank you for covering my accommodations back there," Karnek said.

It would come out of his compensation.

"I've never had a captain who cared if I was covered when we landed. I know you're missing Jarn, but if there's ever anything I can do—*anything*—just ask."

Varik grunted approval, but Karnek would never be in his bed. Not with those teeth. Varik liked to bite, and if Karnek decided to bite back... Varik's insides shriveled at the image.

"Can I ask what your plan is to find more crew on Cassan? I'd like to help any way I can."

Karnek was a decent communications officer—he'd found the dark site after all—but it wasn't enough. "We'll find them any way we can. Crews are always available when you know where to look. To pay them, we have to secure new contracts and make credits. As much as we can."

Funds weren't a problem at all. Auvi, his dead lover and former captain of *The Treasure*, had left Varik plenty, but he didn't allow anyone to get lazy on his tab. And there was no such thing as too many credits. *And* if some of those contracts they secured were intended to go to *The Treasure*? Even better. If he couldn't blow the ship up, he could at least starve out the crew. Cyra deserved it for stealing what belonged to him.

"Excellent." Karnek grinned, and his razor teeth made Varik's stomach turn. One of the new crew members better be attractive enough and willing to see to Varik's needs. Auvi had never had any trouble securing a willing partner, and Varik was twice the male that weakling had ever been. "As soon as we're in range, I'll post on the board for crew and check for any contracts, Captain."

"Good." Varik released his harness.

"Captain?"

Varik paused in his retreat.

"I just want to thank you for taking a chance on me. Trusting me. My people get a bad rap as being...well, you know. But you hired me anyway. And now that it's just you and me, I'll repay that trust, earn that trust every single moment."

Varik turned and lifted his lips in a smile. "I'm counting on it."

CHAPTER 4

Blaize dragged her hand across her neck under her tied-up hair. A bead of sweat trailed from her forehead down the side of her face. The engine room wasn't overly hot, but she'd been on edge since leaving Kolben. There was nothing she could pinpoint. After a perfect takeoff, their fuel-burn rate was within normal parameters. She'd checked every system report twice, inspected every manual gauge, and crawled through every crevice of the ship's heart she could reach. Nothing was wrong.

Except for the itchy sensation that wouldn't leave her alone. The dread that something was about to blow. Maybe it was her reaction to Dez removing a bomb from the outside of her engine and losing his hand. Maybe it was Cyra's apprehension about taking the ER bridge bleeding into Blaize. Or her threat to add to engineering staff. Perhaps it was the sensation of someone watching her. The eerie foreboding had hit somewhere in the cargo bay and hadn't left her since.

It was probably just too quiet. "I think I'll check out the stats on the rotating detonator. You know, the way it's designed on *The Treasure* is quite odd." She wasn't speaking to anyone, but the sound calmed her. "Emotional energy is transferred from the bridge apparatus through the converter, concentrated, and burst-delivered right to the rotator, causing the spin needed to create the detonation. The RoDRE is technically pretty antiquated technology, but whoever originally designed *The Treasure* was brilliant. The fuel savings are astronomical. Never having to burn fuel to punch out of the atmosphere is huge, especially with a ship this large. I'm kind of impressed Cyra could pull it off without Dez working her to climax on the bridge. I could die without seeing that. I mean, Dez and the captain are beautiful together, his dark striped skin and hers—that deep blue, nearly purple. I mean, who wouldn't want to see them together? But not like that. I wouldn't be able to unsee his dick. I mean, I like dicks, but his dick is taken."

Was that a snort?

Blaize spun around, searching for the source of the sound.

"Who's there? Show yourself."

Nothing moved.

"Approaching the KolFlamm wormhole," Rhysa's voice rang out from Blaize's comm.

"Acknowledged." Blaize glanced around the crowded room once more. Nothing moved. As it shouldn't. She turned her back and headed to the bridge to strap in for the crossing. With any luck, they wouldn't experience a time shift—big or small—but there were no guarantees. Wormholes made long-distance travel possible, but not without unpredictable costs.

She rubbed the back of her neck. Maybe her foreboding had nothing to do with the engines and everything to do with a future catastrophe. Rhysa and Bodi were in their usual places on the bridge. Calm. Professional. Veda had taken one of the empty chairs near Bodi. Blaize dropped into the empty one next to Rhysa and tugged the safety harness, securing herself for the inexplicable experience of ER bridge crossings. No two had been the same, and she braced for the unexpected.

"Did you warn Captain Cyra?" Blaize asked the team.

"Nope." Rhysa lips lifted in a wicked grin. "Dez said not to disturb them. Their mating ritual is pretty involved from what I read. She probably doesn't know she's on *The Treasure* by now, much less care if we're crossing a bridge."

Lucky captain.

"Do you think the plants will be okay?" Veda asked.

"Of course." Blaize had no idea how the plants would react to the crossing, but there was nothing to be done about it and no point in upsetting her. "You gave them a very secure structure."

"Notice of crossing sent." Bodi's only sign of nerves was a slight fluttering of her transparent, vestigial wings. "Proceed when ready."

The fact that the crew followed all the safety protocols without resistance pleased Blaize. The rules were there for a reason, but she'd worked with crews who believed the old laws to be overkill.

"Penetrating the hole now." Rhysa's gleeful double entendre made Veda snort laugh.

At least someone was having fun. Blaize took several slow, deep breaths and braced herself for the entrance, which would be slightly worse than the exit. Wormholes sucked. Literally. Blaize swallowed her stomach back down as it seemed to lift into her throat. The familiar, but unwelcome, tugging and slight disorientation came next. She forced herself to slow her breathing and remember that *The Treasure* was designed for this type of travel. Even though it was her first crossing on the transport, it was a solid ship. She'd been over it with a fine-tooth comb. Nothing would go wrong. And with any luck, they wouldn't be too far out of sync with time.

She slowed her breathing to a normal rhythm and closed her eyes. The swirling colors on the viewscreens disoriented her enough to be uncomfortable. Finally, the telltale tugging returned. Or, really, intensified.

"Pulling out," Rhysa called.

With a stutter, they returned to the standard view of stars, and the physical stretch stopped.

"No time lapse," Bodi responded.

"Yeah!" Rhysa held out her hand, and Bodi slapped her palm.

"Nice job, Nav." Bodi returned her attention to her station. "Sending cross complete now."

"Coordinates for Cassan are in." Rhysa spun in her chair with a satisfied smile. Blaize shot her an approving smile and nod, but there really wasn't much navigating once the ship entered the ER bridge. The hole did whatever it wanted with the ship, and you prayed it all went well. Mostly it did. But still, everyone liked to receive approval for a job well done.

"I'm also sending a message to Cassan that we're on track for deliveries."

A hint of foreboding prickled the back of Blaize's neck. The sensation of something being not quite right. "Can you scan for Varik's ship, too?"

"Already on it," Bodi replied without looking up.

"Yeah, that fucker is going down for what he did to Dez and almost did to *The Treasure*. I know guys who would hate-fuck his eye socket for me." Rhysa's pink eyes flared red. For a tiny thing, she was frightening on occasion. Also, who had she been dating?

"Better than he deserves." Veda freed herself from the safety straps.

Blaize blinked. She'd never heard Veda sound bloodthirsty before. It was like discovering a bunny had fangs.

"I'd watch that on loop," Bodi added.

"I'm with Veda—better than he deserves." But Blaize

wouldn't watch it. The idea of looking at him turned her stomach. She freed herself from her seat. "I'm off to safety check the engines."

"Blaize?" Veda paused at the door to the bridge. "Do you have a minute to help me with the plants?"

"Sure thing." Checking the engines after the crossing was a safety habit, like Bodi sending the entrance and exit communication blasts. Highly unlikely anything was wrong, so no rush.

CHAPTER 5

Cifer pressed into the spare space at the edge of the engine room, a quivering mess of flesh. Wormholes always left him disoriented, as if pieces of his body weren't quite connected, but the experience had been particularly unpleasant without the benefit of a secured position. Footsteps in the corridor forced him to ignore his physical difficulties and resume his camouflage—easier imagined than executed in his current state.

"Did you survive?" Blaize's voice barely reached him. Was she speaking to him? Could she see him? He opened his eyes and did a visual check of his concealment. It was perfect. How could she see him?

"In you go. Back in your crate." A yip echoed.

Blaize was speaking to the puppy, not him. He'd learned Blaize's name from the other crew member, the one in charge of the greenhouse.

A few moments later, her voice filled the room. "Hello, handsome. Did you miss me? I know that had to be traumatic for you. But I'm going to mix a special blend of lubricant and make sure all your parts are in full working order."

What?

"You did such a good job of getting us across the bridge. Perfectly executed."

Cifer swallowed a chuckle. She was talking to the engine as if it were alive. Cabinet doors snicked close, the secure latches necessary to keep the contents inside, especially in situations like they'd just experienced. At least he'd learned as a youth— mainly through violence at the hands of his captors—not to puke after a crossing, but the urge remained a close thing.

Blaize continued to babble at her systems. Her words were difficult to hear clearly as she moved around the equipment, but though the tones were muffled, he still enjoyed them. A ping drew his attention from the sultry voice. A nut. Cifer's tail shot out to retrieve it before he could resist. He toyed with it briefly before tucking it in a pocket of his pouch, next to the orb.

"That's better, isn't it? Nice and slick. Feels so good."

Cifer was willing to confirm her assessment.

"Let me give you a squeeze." The female's voice was practically in his ear. His cock responded to the offer.

Her stunning red hair caught his eye again. He hadn't exaggerated the vibrancy in his imagination— she was every bit as bright as he'd remembered. Her luminous pale skin was the perfect canvas to accentuate her vibrancy. Even the icy blue of her eyes was so pale as to be nearly nonexistent. Cifer clenched his hands to fists to keep from reaching for her. No matter how her curves begged to be held, her full lips to be kissed, his contract took priority. *The Treasure* could make the journey to Hiargus. If he could sneak off the ship on Cassan and then contract the captain to take him, there'd be no issue. But that plan depended on him staying hidden, not riding this beautiful female to completion over and over again. Maybe after he negotiated for paid passage, he could risk pursuing an affair.

An eerie metallic scrape dragged Cifer's mind out of the

future and the possibility of pleasure. Blaize continued to babble. Another scraping sound compelled Cifer to abandon his no-movement policy. He craned his neck, searching for the source.

Above where Blaize worked, a light tilted at an odd angle. Before he could decide what to do, a nut pinged to the floor. The large metal fixture slid away from its mount.

Cifer leaped forward, stretching his arms to reach for the flying metal hazard headed straight for Blaize. He bashed the huge fixture to the side with one hand and tugged Blaize out of danger with the other.

Blaize screeched and pummeled his chest.

He discarded a layer of his camouflage. "Are you—"

She wriggled in his grip, and he released her. "Who are you? What did you do? I could have been killed."

Cifer blinked. She was *angry* with him? He held up his hands in surrender. "That's why I saved you."

"You aren't authorized to be on this ship. How did you get on board, and what are you doing in the engine room? How long have you been here? I'm calling security."

Cifer considered which question to answer first while he savored the intense beauty of the female yelling at him. He'd held her curves only for a single moment, but he would never forget the experience. She was lush layers over solid strength. An ideal he didn't know existed before.

"Blaize? Are you okay? What happened?"

The voice startled Cifer out of his lusty haze, and he shifted his coloring to hide. The short brown gardener appeared. Cifer froze.

"Blaize?"

"Do you see him, Veda?" Blaize swiveled her neck, eyes frantic. "He was just here."

"Who?"

"The person who saved me." Blaize pointed at the broken light fixture.

"You could have died." Veda glanced from the fixture Cifer had knocked away to the ceiling where the ballast should have been.

"Show yourself," Blaize demanded, still searching.

"I don't know who you are or why you're on this ship, but you saved my friend's life, so thank you." Veda directed her words over his left shoulder.

One person knowing he existed was a problem. Two meant he could no longer remain hidden. His cover was blown. "I would prefer to remain concealed. I need a ride to Cassan, nothing more. I'm no threat to you or anyone on this ship."

"Are you escaping from Kolben? Are you a miner? I can understand why someone would risk stowing away, but that's still not—" Blaize shook her head, obviously still rattled.

"The ride I purchased to get off Kolben left without me, and I have a contractual obligation that requires me elsewhere."

Veda wrinkled her nose. "It's a little weird talking to the wall and hearing it respond. Please reveal yourself."

He slowly revealed the version of himself he used in public.

"The only reason we were on Kolben was to deliver Dez. Thankfully, we didn't have to leave him, because that place is horrible." Veda inspected him, gaze trailing a methodical path over his person, no emotion.

"I agree." The atrocious conditions for the miners bordered on criminal. He hadn't wanted to spend one more second there than he had to. As soon as he could, he would look into what he could do to help them.

Blaize crossed her arms and glared at him. "Now that I know you're on the ship, not just suspecting—because I did think someone might be on the ship, but I also considered it might be my imagination— I have to tell the captain."

Icy fear, almost as cold as space, washed through him. "I wish you wouldn't. I won't be any trouble."

"Cyra and Dez are fair." Veda gave him a reassuring smile that didn't ease his concerns.

"I'm sure they are, but stowaways are generally dealt with by ejecting them out the nearest portal." Cifer had seen it once in his youth, and he'd never forgotten. "I'd prefer not to end my trip by becoming space dust prematurely."

"You saved my life. But you did stow away, and technically that does make you a criminal. But they wouldn't..." Blaize trailed off.

"They likely would. I was avoiding certain death on Kolben, and my travel is on behalf of another planet whose inhabitants will suffer greatly if I don't complete my journey. Please, for them, would you keep my presence a secret?" He might be slightly exaggerating about the importance of the orb. But maybe not. He wasn't familiar with the species of humans that occupied Hiargus.

"If they find out we knew..." Veda shook her head.

"I won't be found. I'm very good at hiding."

Blaize dusted off her hands on the pant legs of the coveralls. "I'm obligated to tell the Security Officer."

Cifer's gaze locked on to the female as she marched away. A storm of beauty that made his heart pound. He couldn't chase her, wouldn't try, and shouldn't be tempted to seduce her. She was the type of woman who, once he made her his, he would be unable to leave. And that didn't fit with his lifestyle.

"I'll stay with you." Veda's voice brought him back to the engine room. "It'll be okay. You'll see."

Cifer very much doubted it would be, but he was out of moves.

"Do you want to see my greenhouse?"

Didn't really matter how he spent his final moments on the

ship, and the hopeful pride in Veda's voice couldn't be ignored. Rather than confess to eating a bit of her harvest, he said. "I would. I've never seen a greenhouse on a ship before. How does that work with the rigors of space?"

Veda gave him a warm smile tinged with surprise. "It wouldn't work on just any ship, but *The Treasure* was designed for bio-transport. Between that and the special growing methods I'm using, I'm seeing significant production rates."

She prattled on as Cifer followed her amongst the plants. But his mind was on the beautiful female he'd held for a perfect moment. The one who would expedite his certain death.

CHAPTER 6

Blaize and Dez strode down the corridor toward the engine room, not speaking. As they got to the opening to Veda's greenhouse, Dez held his hand up, and she stopped. He froze and tilted his head like he could hear something. Blaize couldn't hear anything but the usual ship whirring and hissing, a low background noise she'd come to associate with all systems normal. Dez held up his hand again and mouthed the word, *Stay*. She nodded, and he slinked toward the greenhouse so silently that no one would hear him coming.

"Veda." Dez's voice boomed through the doorway which he filled.

Blaize moved closer, but quietly, so she didn't draw the big man's wrath.

"Where did he go?" Dez didn't move from the door, but his head was swiveling, peering into the room in all directions. Blaize tried to see around him, but all she caught was a brief glimpse of Veda, whose brow was wrinkled as she bit her lip.

"Veda. Where did that man go?"

"Um..." Veda sounded like she was about to cry. "Please don't be mad. He saved Blaize's life."

"Where is he?" Dez's voice was so loud, Blaize jumped back and crashed into the far wall of the corridor. He turned his glare on her. "I told you to wait."

Blaize didn't move. She was prey, and he was in full predator mode. Freezing might not be wise, but it was instinctual.

"This is Cifer." Veda spoke as soon as Dez turned back to the room.

Blaize crept up beside him so she could see in. There stood the impressive male who'd rescued her. Copper skin highlighted his brown eyes with flecks of green. Long brown hair fell just past his very wide shoulders. He wasn't as tall as Dez, but he was thick with muscles. She had a strange impulse to ask him to remove his shirt.

"Furcifer Msuya. Cifer." The stowaway held out his hand.

Dez growled. His normally gray skin had a red cast, and his yellow eyes practically glowed. She'd never heard him make that sound or look so angry.

Cifer was in big trouble. She had to say something. "Dez, he saved my life. He had to get off Kolben. I know it looks bad, but—"

"Blaize, it more than *looks* bad. It *is* bad. He's a stowaway." Dez shook his head. "Veda. Showing him around? Really? And Blaize, why did you wait so long to tell me your concerns?"

"She didn't know I was on board until after the ER jump. A fixture came loose from the ceiling."

"Did I ask you to speak?" Dez puffed up even larger, blocking Blaize's view completely. "Give me one reason I shouldn't eject you right now."

"I can pay, for my transport. I didn't have the luxury of negotiating passage while I was on the planet, but I'm more than able to cover the cost of my travel."

Blaize found herself believing everything Cifer said and wanting to hear more. But the last time she'd been enamored by a male, he had stolen her ship out from under her. She couldn't trust her own judgment. Maybe Dez *should* space Cifer out the airlock.

"Dez, we can put him in the cargo hold. Talk about it with Cyra?" Veda was begging.

"I'm the security officer. I don't require the captain's approval to deal with security violations that threaten the safety of this crew."

"But he didn't threaten our safety. He *saved* my life." Blaize clenched her jaw shut to keep from rattling on.

"His presence is a threat."

"You didn't even know he was here." Veda's voice carried into the hallway. She was never that loud.

"That's exactly my point, Veda," Dez barked back at her.

"Please, can we talk it over with the captain and the crew? He's a good guy," Veda begged.

Were they being taken in by a gorgeous male with a sexy voice who'd done one good deed? For all Blaize knew, the guy had engineered the accident so he could save her and make her his advocate.

"I'm more than willing to be placed in whatever holding cell you deem appropriate if you would please consider my offer. I can pay premium prices. I have no intention of harming anyone or being a burden of any kind."

That voice. It caressed Blaize's back and stroked her hair. She fell so easily under his spell. She shook her head and opened her mouth to offer her reformed opinion to Dez: eject the stowaway.

"Fine. You can stay in the locked cargo hold while we discuss the matter with the captain. We have security feeds in that area. If you do anything that I deem a threat, those will be your last actions inside this ship."

"I understand. Thank you." Cifer's conciliatory tone might be just another manipulation, but it sounded convincing.

Blaize stuffed her fists into the pockets of her coveralls and stomped down to the engine room. Working on the systems would help her calm down and get over whatever power that male had with his voice. Apparently it worked on males, too. Otherwise, how would he have convinced Dez to compromise?

"Blaize, meet us in the galley," Dez called to her.

She waved acknowledgment, but she had to inspect the light fixture first.

Blaize slumped into a chair in the galley, frustrated with the interruption. Her emotions swirled, disrupting any logical thought she attempted. She didn't know anything about the Cifer guy, except he was a criminal stowaway and he'd saved her life. She huffed and balled her hands into fists in her pockets.

Veda fussed with the hot drink dispenser. For some reason, the medic prepared tea for any difficult discussion. There was no tea on Blaize's childhood planet, and the inhabitants had survived plenty of difficult discussions—mostly. Veda placed the steaming cup in front of her. It would be bad manners to ignore it.

"Thanks, Veda." She removed her hands from her pockets and wrapped them around the drink. The warmth seeping into her hands and up her arms did feel good. She took a deep breath. Maybe Veda had a point after all.

Dez and Cyra were the last ones to join the meeting. Dez ignored his tea and remained standing.

"There's been a security incident on the ship. We have an unauthorized passenger currently being held in the cargo hold."

"What? How is this possible?" Bodi's voice was shrill and her face pale. Her hands trembled slightly, and her wings twitched as she reached for her tea.

"There was a window where we were awaiting the fuel delivery and cargo loads, and everyone was otherwise occupied. The loading bay was left unattended. I was assured by the dock master when we landed that the ship would be guarded at all times, but I think we know that wasn't the case." Dez's voice remained calm but tight.

Not even close. Blaize crossed her arms and curled in on herself. She should have been more vigilant.

Cyra gave his hand a quick squeeze before letting him go again.

"We can't fix the breach, but we need to decide what action we are taking with him."

"Him? Is he cute?" Rhysa bounced a little in her seat.

Blaize glared at Rhysa to no effect.

"He's very kind." Veda sat down finally. "He saved Blaize's life."

"What? Your life was threatened?" Bodi snapped her attention to Blaize.

"There was a loose light in the engine room. Must have come loose during the jump, and it gave way, but he kept it from crashing into me."

Bodi shuddered but said nothing.

"How do you know it was the jump? Couldn't he have sabotaged the light?" Rhysa asked.

"Why would you assume that?" Veda's eyebrows were pinched.

"I'm not assuming anything. He could be an assassin for all we know."

"An assassin?" Bodi gasped. Her wings buzzed. Definitely not the party girl Blaize knew.

"He's not an assassin." Veda's voice was louder than Blaize had ever heard it. She had to explain.

"In addition to the light fixture being so high it would require a hoist to get to it, it would be difficult to predict where I would be in the engine room when the light fixture failed. If he's an assassin, he sucks. Besides, I think he's trying to steal a ride, not kill anyone. He's been on the ship for cycles, and there've been no problems." Other than him watching her as she did her job. Did he watch her at other times? The hair on her arms raised. "I don't know. Maybe he's an escaped miner, but I mean, who wouldn't want to get away from that place? He says he's working a contract for another planet."

"Blaize has a very good point," Dez spoke over her words as they continued to spew out of her mouth. "It is unlikely that he is on the ship to intentionally harm anyone. Otherwise, why prevent the accident?" Dez's focus was on Bodi.

"But he's still a stowaway." Bodi turned the teacup in her hands.

"He is. And we are well within our rights to eject him. Honestly, it was my gut response." Dez's voice was gentle but firm, and his yellow eyes traveled over each of them. "As the crew, and Cyra's partners, it is appropriate for you each to have a say in what happens to him."

"The extra weight on the ship will impact my fuel calculations, and he will need to be fed." Blaize offered up the facts as calmly as possible. "Will that hurt our food reserves?" The vote needed to consider all the variables, not just the fact that Cifer's voice made her want to melt.

"Valid points." Rhysa tapped her lip with her forefinger.

"Are we so tight on fuel that the added hundred kilos will create a problem?" Cyra asked.

"No." Heat burned Blaize's cheeks. "But it's not free."

"As for food, my queen—er, the captain—worries I don't eat enough." Blaize thought Dez's slip was cute but held back her grin. "I believe we have sufficient stores should he prove to be ravenous." It was obvious he wanted to be professional, but hell, with the way the ship had to be boosted to make it out of atmosphere, *everyone* was on intimate terms with Cyra—at least as a voyeur.

"Has he told you why he's on the ship?" Rhysa asked.

Usually, it made Blaize a little nuts the way the navigation officer questioned authority. But the decision to kill someone shouldn't be taken lightly, no matter how big a rule they broke.

"He has not explained his presence, but he did offer to pay for his transportation." Dez's voice gave no indication of how he would decide the issue.

"What if he was part of the plan to set the bomb?" Bodi's translucent wings were fluttering so fast they were a blur. Was she aware of it?

"The bomb did almost kill you. And it was meant for *The Treasure*. What if he snuck on board to finish the job?" Blaize shuddered. Having a murderer on board was as bad as the poisonous spiders. If the cargo didn't improve, she might have to seek employment elsewhere, no matter how well she might fit in with the crew.

"Then why would he save you?" Veda asked. "If he's trying to kill the crew or destroy the ship, he wouldn't have risked injury—or being ejected from the ship—to save anyone. He could have blown us up during the crossing, and any investigation would have written it off as an anomaly in the ER bridge."

"I sensed no violence from him during our initial meeting or when I escorted him to the cargo hold." Dez had nearly been killed saving the ship and had lost his hand. If he didn't think the guy was the bomber, then he was probably correct.

Captain Cyra raised her arm, and everyone shut up. "I think we should take a vote."

"Yes, my captain." Dez nodded in Cyra's direction. "Should we keep the stowaway in cargo until we reach Cassan? Or eject him?"

"Keep him." Veda's voice was the loudest Blaize had ever heard.

"Eject." Bodi hung her head after her quiet vote.

"Rhysa?" Dez asked.

"Keep him. I'm sure we can find some use for him." Her tone said exactly how she could imagine using him. A twinge of jealousy caught Blaize unexpectedly.

"My vote is to eject. The security risk is great. It's my job to protect the captain, the crew, and this ship." Dez's vote surprised Blaize. She'd expected him to go easier on the guy based on the discussion.

"Blaize?" At Cyra's call, the entire crew turned to focus on her.

She took a deep breath. Her vote would break the tie. No pressure. Just a person's life. A person who had saved her life. "I think we should keep him in the cargo hold. I'm not convinced he isn't a criminal, but I can't be responsible for the death of a living being if I'm wrong. And, although stowing away is sufficient justification to eject him based on the law, it just doesn't seem right to me. But no matter how *we* vote, it's the captain's decision, not mine."

Cyra tilted her head back and rubbed her throat, exposing her gills. She sat quietly for several minutes. No one moved or hardly breathed. This was serious. A life hung in the balance.

The bile built in Blaize's stomach the more time passed without her captain's decision. Killing Cifer didn't seem right. It made her head hurt to think about it.

Veda stood, and Blaize flinched at the unexpected movement. The tiny woman placed her cup in the sterilizing unit. She faced the captain with her hands fisted on her hips. Cyra made eye contact with her, and they must have had a silent conversation. Cyra gave a quick nod. "Keep him in holding. Let him know I will expect payment for his transport when we arrive in Cassan, or I will alert the authorities about his unauthorized presence on the ship and his possible involvement with the bomb on Kolben. Although, I think we all know that was Varik."

"Yes, Captain." Dez rose from his seat and held out his hand to Cyra.

She took it, but she released him as soon as she was standing. "I'm going to my tank."

The ship had a specialized water chamber just for the captain, who was born on a water planet and needed the immersion to remain healthy. She often went there in times of stress.

"I will speak to the...guest and then meet you in our quarters, my captain."

Cyra left without another word.

Blaize didn't miss making those kinds of decisions. Being captain was a huge responsibility. Keeping the systems running was enough of a challenge for her.

Bodi left silently too. Blaize hoped they hadn't made the wrong decision.

Blaize swiped the large data screen in front of her seat on the bridge. She'd been rearranging the same data for three cycles, data she'd already submitted to the captain.

"Are you okay?" Rhysa loomed over her, inspecting her like

a bug. Blaize hadn't seen or heard her leave her chair at the helm.

"What?" Blaize did her best innocent look.

"Uh-huh. That's what I thought. You voted to keep him, but now you don't want to go by the cargo hold."

Blaize stiffened her spine and tilted her chin up. "I have no idea what you're talking about."

"Scared?"

"Hardly. I had reports to do." Blaize stepped into Rhysa's space, and the navigator took a step back. "And now I have to check the systems." Even though she didn't want to.

"If you're going to the engine room, would you check on Cifer?" Veda looked up from her spot in the far corner of the bridge. "I spoke to him earlier, but it's been a while. With him locked in, we need to make sure he's okay on a regular basis."

Dammit, she couldn't tell Veda no. She was too nice. Time to face her ridiculous attraction to the stranger. "Sure."

Blaize thumped down the corridor. If Rhysa had left her alone, she could have hidden on the deck for at least a few more hours, if not a few more cycles. Instead, she walked toward the gorgeous stowaway with a come-hither voice. She'd fallen for a sexy male once—had the certificate of completion in her lesson in betrayal. No need for a remedial course.

If she was quick, she could pass by the cell where he was being housed—the same one Dez had occupied so recently—verify the guy was alive, and keep going. Fast. That was the way to do this. Rip off the bandage, and it would be over before she had time to worry or talk to him.

She placed her palm on the access panel. Dez had implemented tighter security, and all the pass-through doors that once remained opened were closed all the time. Once the door slid back, she crossed into the cargo hold.

Once again, Princess, the pup, wasn't in her cage—probably with Cyra. Blaize glanced into the open grate of the first cell and froze. Cifer should be there, lying on the bunk or doing pushups on the floor like Dez had done on the way to Kolben. Instead, the cell was empty. There was nowhere to hide. The bunk was a block, built into the hull of the ship. A flat mattress and thermal cover lay on top. Smooth, no lump, no body, nothing. She backed up a few steps and moved a little closer to the metal enclosure. She could see into the bathing alcove. It was shallow and well lit. He wasn't in there.

With her face pressed between the bars, she looked at every wall, inspected the ceiling and the shadows of the corners. Nothing. She pulled on the door, but it was firmly locked. She spun and, with her back to the cell, looked around the open cargo hold. There wasn't anywhere else to hide. He had to be in the cell. Without considering the wisdom of her plan, she opened the cell door and went inside. As she stared at the bunk, a breeze touched a tendril of her hair. There could be no breeze on a ship. When she felt it again, she reached up, wrapped her hands around the appendage that was too close to her head, and flung the attached body forward and down onto the bunk.

"Oof." Cifer was visible now, splayed on the bunk with his head at the foot, between her parted legs. His greenish-brown eyes twinkled, and a slow smile crossed his face as he stared pointedly at her crotch.

Blaize stepped back and closed her stance but kept her arms in fighting position. "Where the hell where you?"

"There was a screw loose." Cifer pointed to the ceiling. "The rattling was disturbing my rest."

Blaize peeked over her shoulder, and there was a vent cover where he pointed. "It's not rattling now."

"I fixed it."

"Why were you hiding? You had to see me. I looked everywhere before I came in here. I shouldn't have come in. You were trying to get me to come in, weren't you? I should've called Dez as soon as you were missing. Now you're going to kill me or take me hostage or something."

"Whoa, whoa, whoa." Cifer sat up on the edge of the bunk. He held his hands out as if he could stop her talking with his hands alone. "I've never killed anyone. And if I was going to start, it wouldn't be someone as beautiful as you."

She scoffed.

"Besides, I had cycles on the ship before you knew I was here. Don't you think I would have done something then?"

"So you're willing to be a killer? But waiting? Maybe you did rig the light, since you seem to be able to climb on ceilings."

"That's not at all what I said. I told you I'm not a killer."

"But you are a criminal." Blaize took another step back toward the door of the cell.

"I have found myself on the far side of the law a time or two, but it wasn't by choice."

"Of course it was by choice. Everyone has the choice of how they behave. But criminals believe it's always someone else's fault, usually the victim's."

"No, in my case it was never the victim's fault." Cifer leaned forward on his knees. "Others were to blame, but not the victims."

"And now the crew members of *The Treasure* are your victims."

"If I made you feel a victim in any way, I apologize. It is not my intention to take advantage. As I've explained, I'm willing to pay for my passage."

"Like paying for it afterwards makes it better." She put her hands on her hips and glared.

"Sometimes making amends is all you can do." He stood and held out one hand.

Blaize took another step back and tripped over her feet. Cifer shot out an arm and grabbed her hand, saving her again. As soon as his fingers wrapped around hers, she was aware of the mistake. She should never have entered his cell, let him close, or let him touch her. Her heart raced, but it wasn't fear. It was something far more concerning: attraction.

He stepped close to her, so close she could feel the whisper of his breath on her face and the nearness of his body to hers. Her breathing stopped. Heat moved up her arm and down lower, between her legs. Legs that remained unsteady.

"Blaize." His voice caressed her ear. "Your parents blessed you with the perfect name." He wrapped a tendril of her hair around the fingers of his free hand.

She yanked her hand out of his grip and dove through the door of the cell, closing it firmly behind her. She was panting. His fingers slid over her hair, and she leaped away. "What is wrong with you?"

Cifer's eyebrows were pinched, and he frowned at her words. His eyes flashed a vibrant green before returning to the browner color they'd been. "Nothing is wrong with me. And nothing is wrong with you, either."

He saw too much. "You don't know anything about me. I was sent to check on you. You appear fine."

"As do you." His sultry tone teased between her legs.

Blaize snorted and stomped out of the holding area toward her engines. The nerve of Cifer. Her hair was none of his business. That story about the screw was probably total bullshit. There wasn't a screw, nut, or bolt on this ship that she hadn't personally inspected over the past few galactic months.

Before the ER crossing...

Anything could have rattled free like the light fixture.

Was she arguing in his favor once again?

Damn her weak constitution. If she'd voted correctly in the

first place, he'd already be gone, and she wouldn't be questioning her judgment. Except...he'd saved her life. And aside from sneaking on board and being good at hiding, he'd given her no reason not to trust him.

Her attraction to him was the red flag. Could she trust herself?

CHAPTER 7

CIFER RELAXED ON HIS BUNK. She would come soon. After several cycles, he'd figured out that she was trying to be random in her appearances, possibly to catch him doing something he shouldn't. But her random visits weren't so random. Sometime after Veda brought his first meal of the cycle, Blaize would try to quickly traipse through the cargo hold. He would always call out to her, make her pause. The longest he'd had to wait after Veda fed him had been an hour. He was an expert at waiting.

A glimpse of her red hair, so stark against her pale skin and her lush figure, was enough to make the long bouts of boredom tolerable, the echo of her warm voice enough to keep him satisfied until their next meeting.

The sector door slid open, and Cifer hurled himself to the cell door. "Hello, Beauty." He leaned against the bars casually, as if his heart wasn't pounding from being in her presence. He worried the small metal pieces in his pocket, the one sign of his agitation if she knew to look for it. No matter how much he tried, he'd never been able to stop fiddling with the parts he found.

Sadly, she didn't reply, didn't even turn her head in his direction, but he caught the quick glimpse she spared him with her almost white eyes. If they'd had black striations, they would have been identical to his mother's. Or to the memory of his mother's eyes. Beautiful and clear, catching every detail with a quick glance. Blaize's speed increased until she'd passed through the far door. She would be working on the mechanical parts of the ship, adjusting here, polishing there. From what Cifer could tell, the ship was in top shape, but he wasn't an engineer. Maybe the older ship required as many hours as Blaize spent on it.

As soon as she disappeared, he quickly morphed, elongating his body to impossible proportions for anyone who was not his species, and slipped though the opening in the ventilation grate. He camouflaged himself into the metal gray of the ship and slithered, bonelessly, through the duct until he found Blaize. His tail end remained in his room. He could morph his body, but he couldn't shrink it. His mass stayed the same.

Slowly, he thickened, filling the space almost completely. Transitions required massive energy. The closer he was to his true shape, the easier it was for him to maintain.

Blaize held some kind of tool with a probe. She touched a spot on the bundle of cables and then peered at the readout, again and again. He hadn't seen her perform this task yet. By the frown on her face, she wasn't satisfied with the results. "What is wrong? This should be routine," she muttered.

She was quiet compared to other times he'd watched her. Was she sick?

"Dammit. You piece of shit."

Cifer craned his neck to get a better view through the cover. Blaize cursed the probe that had separated into two pieces. Bent over, she searched the floor nearby, spinning in a complete circle.

"Shit." She stood and went to a workbench set up along the far wall. Her back was to Cifer, so her expression was a mystery, but her hands flew through the cabinets and containers. A couple of times, she stopped and pulled a small item from one of the containers, held it against the probe, and then returned it to the container. After several repetitions, she dropped the probe on the table and went toward the door.

Cifer quickly stretched and pulled himself back through the shaft. He completed his return to normal shape right before she hit the cargo hold.

"What were you doing?" She darted up to the cell door, the closest she'd come to him since the first meeting.

"What?"

"I saw you... I saw something. What were you doing?"

"Uh, just fiddling with these parts." He hoped that would be explanation enough.

"Let me see."

He held up the few screws, gears, nuts, and other bits that he was slowly fashioning into what he thought might turn out to be a bird.

Blaize pressed her face closer, and he moved the half-built sculpture toward her. She jumped back. "Where did you get that stuff?"

Cifer shrugged. "Just lying around, here and there."

She narrowed her eyes. "Are you taking pieces of the ship?"

"Nothing that's attached. Just loose bits of fluff."

"What are you making?"

"Not sure yet." He spun the object and watched her reaction.

She lifted her chin and met his gaze. "I lost a screw. To a probe. I need to find a replacement."

"If something here works, it's yours. Obviously." Cifer held up the odd collection.

"Let me grab the probe."

Cifer smiled. If he hurried, he could pull this off. He

dropped the sculpture in progress on the bunk and shot through the ventilation. While Blaize snatched the probe from the work bench, Cifer reached for the screw that had come loose. He tucked it into a pouch of skin and shot back to the cell.

He was sitting on the bunk, trying to slow his breathing, when she arrived at his cell. The screw she needed didn't connect to the sculpture that would more than likely become a bird, but he stuck it into a hole and gave it a quick twist.

"I have it." She held up the two pieces.

"You can come in." Cifer didn't move from the bunk.

Blaize hesitated, and he was afraid she might refuse. Slowly, she lifted her hand to the control panel, and the door slid open. Cifer raised his eyes and patted the mattress next to him before going back to his sculpture. Blaize sat, farther away than he would have liked, but she'd joined him on the bed. He'd take the small token of trust.

"May I see the probe?"

Blaize gathered it in one hand and held it out to him. Cifer carefully placed the sculpture between them, away from the edge of the bunk. He took the probe from her hands and made a good show of inspecting it as if he was analyzing what part might fit in the connector from the handheld base to the dangling bit of metal used to take the readings.

"It's old, I know. There's way newer technology than this. But it was given to me. I have to fix it. I can't get another one until we reach Cassan, and I really don't want another one. It's the one I learned on—system maintenance, I mean, not just the probe. Do you think you might have a part that would work?"

Cifer waited in case she continued to speak. He loved the sound of her voice. It was like a warm fire on a winter cycle that he recalled from his childhood. Smoky and heated. He imagined them curled up in his bed on Cassan, her talking or reading aloud, anything, just as long as her voice continued to flow.

She remained quiet.

"I'm sure I have something that will work." He handed her the probe and picked up the sculpture. The piece he removed was the wrong one, but he needed more time with her. He held out his palm, and she took the screw from him carefully, avoiding contact.

"It doesn't fit." Her shoulders slumped, and she handed him the unworkable part. Their fingers grazed. She twitched away from him. So, she felt it, too—the electric heat that narrowed his world to her.

"Hold on." Cifer moved his hand near her hair. "I think I see something."

Blaize reached up to her head, but Cifer moved before she could touch him and held open his hand with the screw she needed.

"Nice trick." She took the piece from his open hand without touching him.

He held himself still, not giving himself away with a knowing smile.

"It works. You had it. How did you have a part that fits this old thing? This is so good. You don't even know. Thank you, Cifer." She threw herself into his arms and gave him a firm hug.

"Blaize?" Dez's concerned voice ricocheted through the cell.

Cifer was barely able to wrap his arms briefly around her before she gave him a horrified look and launched herself off the bunk and out of his cell. The scent of her, spicy and floral, lingered along with the heat of her body.

"What were you doing?" Dez asked her.

Cifer didn't care what she answered, as long as she came back.

"I...uh...had to fix this." Blaize held up her probe.

Dez glanced from Cifer to Blaize and back.

"A small screw," Cifer added.

Dez scowled.

Cifer held up the small sculpture he'd been fiddling with. "Happened to have the one she needed."

The door slid shut, and he forced himself to speak before she left. "Will you come back?"

She and Dez paused.

"I'd like to help you with any other small repairs you may have or possibly to share a meal. It's a little tedious in here by myself." And terribly lonely.

Blaize glanced toward her engine room and back. Hesitation froze her in place. Cifer held his breath. She glanced at the big gray security officer.

He shrugged.

"Um, sure. Yes. Of course." She turned as red as her hair. Her white eyes shone when she looked at him. "I do have some repairs, and it must be boring."

Cifer gave her an easy smile.

"I'll bring lunch and tell you what I have." She rushed off.

Dez watched her go, and jealousy poked Cifer in the gut. His world had shrunk to the brief moments when he could see Blaize. The first time he'd been able to get her to come inside, to touch him, and Dez had to show up and ruin it.

"You hurt her, I'll end you. No discussion. No vote. No hesitation."

Cifer's eyes flicked, a momentary loss of control. Dez's eyes widened. He hadn't missed the slip. "I would never harm another being for any reason, but especially not Blaize."

Dez's gaze bored into him, assessing. A short grunt was the only acknowledgement he gave before turning and leaving.

Cifer lay back in his bunk and waited. The orb glowed a

little brighter from its hiding spot in the vent. Any lighter, and he'd have to find another hiding spot. The stupid ball had been dark for cycles. He had no idea why it was activating, but it probably meant he had a closing window of time to return it to the royal family. Too bad there wasn't a thing he could do to speed his return. He hadn't even been able to let the royal family know he'd successfully retrieved it. He sighed. One step at a time. Patience was his best tool.

Blaize returned with lunch, a simple fare of protein and starch elevated with a delicious sauce and a smattering of fresh peppers from Veda's greenhouse.

Cifer licked his utensil clean. "What is this flavor?"

"Dez's family owns a farm on Din' Gale. They sent us with food when we left to take Dez to Kolben."

"Why would you take Dez from Din' Gale to Kolben?" Cifer couldn't imagine two larger extremes of condition, and he wouldn't mind a trip to the lush Din' Gale. He'd only read about it.

"It's a long story. But it all worked out, except for his hand." Blaize stood and took Cifer's bowl from him. "I'll be back."

She returned a while later with several small assemblies in need of repair.

"This one seems to need a bit of adhesive." Cifer spun the stripped screw.

"I think the previous engineer overtightened it and it broke. I don't really have anything that will work. Thread tape fills the gap, but it needs something with some stick."

"What about some spiderweb?"

"Spiderweb?"

"There's a bit in the corridor, up in the corner. It might work."

Blaize went out of his cell and turned to go to the corridor to the greenhouse.

"No, the other way."

She turned around but tilted her head and looked at him strangely.

"I moved around a bit before you caught me." He gave a half-smile with a hint of guilt.

Blaize had to retrieve a small stepstool to reach the sticky web.

He helped her wrap it around the remaining threads and fit it to the hole.

"It works. A perfect fix." She gave him a happy smile. "At least temporarily, until I can get replacement parts."

Cifer's heart pounded with her approval.

Each cycle, Blaize found items Cifer could help her with, usually after a meal. After a few cycles, there were no more small projects she could take to him. For some reason, the lack of time together made her uncomfortable. Probably because he was bored and lonely and locked up. The more she got to know him, the more uncomfortable she was with keeping him in a cage. Perhaps she could find a way to fix that.

"Dez?" Blaize entered the galley where the big gray male cooked with such ease, as if he hadn't recently lost a hand.

"This about Cifer?" he asked without looking up from the pan.

"Well, you know he's been helping me. Small repairs, but I could use an extra hand to do some efficiency tests..." She trailed off. Did she really just tell Dez she needed an extra hand? Her cheeks heated. So insensitive.

"You need more of his help."

She bristled at the word "need." It would be possible to

accomplish the task without assistance, but more risky and slower. "Not *need*. But he's very clever. And strong."

Dez faced her. His yellow-eyed gaze seemed to cut through her layers to parts of her she didn't care to examine.

"Never mind." She spun, intending to retreat.

"Wait."

Dez's command halted her steps.

"It's fine. We'll be at Cassan soon. I'm sure I can get—" She cut off the word help, regretting her decision to come to Dez in the first place.

"You trust him to help you?"

"I do. We've been working in his cell on assemblies I could bring to him. He hasn't made any threatening moves. And if I'm honest, I'm pretty sure he can get out of his cell somehow, although the door is never unlocked and nothing is ever out of place, but he knows things. Maybe from when he was on the ship before we put him in the cell, but I'm not sure. He just seems bored and—"

"It's your decision."

"What about Cyra?"

"She trusts her partners. You have our best interests at heart."

If only Dez would decide and take the pressure off her. If she let Cifer out and something happened, she'd feel horrible. But she'd spent cycles with him, or at least parts of cycles. And he was always respectful and non-threatening. It could be a ruse, but for what?

They were nearly at Cassan. He had everything to lose if he did something dumb and the crew decided to space him.

Once they got there, she might never see him again. The fact that it mattered if she saw him again after they landed disturbed her, but not as much as the idea of not seeing him.

On the station, Cyra would be able to recruit another engineer if she didn't think Blaize could handle the job. Better to have everything in working order and as perfect as she could get it. Dez couldn't safely help her. Veda was too short and busy with her plants and Dez's medical care. Bodi and Rhysa would help in an emergency, but not with cycle-to-cycle stuff. They had their own jobs.

She sighed. Her decision. Her stomach reminded her how it felt to cross a wormhole. "I'll test it. See how it goes."

"I'm one heartbeat away. And I can take him, one-handed." Dez grinned at her over his shoulder.

"Right," she agreed, unsure if he meant for her to laugh. "I'll...uh..." Leave before she said anything stupid.

Blaize paused outside the cargo bay door. She had to get her head straight before she tried to speak to Cifer. There was something about him that made logic fly out the porthole. Princess's crate was empty. Cyra kept the thuringy with her more and more lately. But that meant Blaize couldn't avoid her decision by playing with the pup.

Cifer stretched out in the cell, doing pushups without a shirt on. His muscles were pumped, and he'd probably been at the activity for a while. He sped up and then added a clap. When she expected him to quit, he started doing one hand for a two count and then the other. She wasn't sure how long she watched him, a tightness winding between her legs.

"Have you seen enough, Beauty? Or would you like more?"

Blaize turned away and sucked in a breath. Cifer's chuckle had her turning back with anger instead of embarrassment. "You knew I was here."

"Of course. You tend to stomp. Especially when you're angry." He stepped to the door and gripped the bars. "What have I done now?"

Sweat made his warm skin glow, like copper in the sun. She shook her head. Damn, he was distracting. "Nothing."

"Then why are you angry with me?" He reached for a lock of her hair.

She stepped back. "I'm not. I'm trying to make a decision."

"Can I help decide?"

"It's about you."

"Damn, are we back to spacing me already?" His eyes went soft, and she swore he pouted.

"No." She crossed her arms. "I'm considering if I can trust you or not."

He pressed his body against the bars of the door. "Of course you can. I'm very good with secrets. What do you want to tell me?"

"It's not a secret." Why was this so difficult? "I came to ask you if you'd be interested in helping me in engineering?"

Cifer stepped back. "I've *been* helping you. Not that you need it."

Did his cell brighten, or was it the surprise of someone recognizing that she was good at her job? She dropped her arms and took a step forward. "I could use a hand. Occasionally. In the engine room and the other system areas."

Cifer didn't respond. She figured he'd jump on the idea. Maybe it was a bad offer. Maybe he wanted compensation. Maybe he didn't want to work with her.

"Thank you."

"What does that mean?" she snapped. "I mean, if you don't want to, I understand. It's not like a job or anything, but I'm out of—" She stopped.

He grinned as if he'd won something. "I would be honored to help you in *any way I can*, Beauty."

Ugh. Why did he make the offer sound so sexual? And why did she like it? "It's Blaize. And one misstep, one red flag, and you'll be back in this cell for the duration. Don't make me regret this offer."

She spun on her heel and retreated to her quarters. If this decision cost her credibility with her business partners, she'd never forgive Cifer or herself. But that wasn't as likely as falling even harder for his charms. She laughed at herself as she flopped onto the bed. Who was she kidding? She'd already succumbed.

CHAPTER 8

"Captain?"

Varik roused from half-slumber to sit straighter in his captain's chair in the center of the bridge. "What is it?"

"I found *The Treasure*. Or at least I found their docking request." Karnek grinned, his teeth more off-putting than usual. "They're stopping at Cassan with a delivery."

"When?" Maybe he could reach the space station before that lumbering behemoth Cyra stole from him. "We have to be there first."

Karnek's smile faded. "We're tracking to get there a cycle later."

"Fix it."

"But I'm a communications exp—"

Varik stood. "And I'm an engineer. But I'm also the captain."

"Yes, Captain. I'll get the computer to run some scenarios."

"Anything else?"

"No." Karnek pounded away on the keys, his head hanging.

"You said they were making a delivery?" Varik tried for a more approving tone. Despite what he'd told Karnek earlier, it was tough finding good help.

Karnek slid a few screens off-view and brought up a manifest. One he shouldn't be able to see. Maybe the communications expert had some value after all. "Small load from Kolben. Six crew. One passenger. One service animal."

Service animal? "Wait, passenger?"

"Yes, sir. No name, but definitely says passenger. That ship is rated for universal transport. Few mods, and it could be a pleasure cruiser." Karnek waggled his thick brows.

Varik clenched his jaw. Could have been *his* pleasure cruiser. But the passenger. And six crew members. "Can you pull up their manifest from when they left Cassan?"

Karnek leaned forward, fingers flying.

"Four crew, one humanoid transport."

Varik paced across the short distance of the bridge and back. Cyra, the filthy whore. Veda, the bowl of pudding. Doc had retired. Blaize, the traitorous cunt. The pink-eyed freak. And a contracted delivery to Kolben. Humanoid.

Jarn had to be on *The Treasure*. There was no other explanation. He was alive. Varik's chest ballooned. His steps lightened. He hadn't killed his lover. Again.

"Alright, what's the computer found? How fast can we get to Cassan? I don't care how much fuel we burn. Any scenario."

Karnek sat straighter and clicked away. "Three possible options."

"Bring them fullscreen."

The viewscreen that showed the stars and vast blackness of space shifted to an opaque white display before three maps were displayed, tiled next to each other. Varik closed in on the screen, examining each option. He stepped back to see all three at once.

"Fuel variance ten percent," he called out.

A red overlay appeared on the second image. "That one. Program that route."

"Another ER bridge?" Karnek grimaced. "But—"

Varik glared at him, letting the man's death fill his eyes.

"Yes, Captain."

Varik left the bridge and locked himself in his quarters. Jarn. His lover was alive and would be in his arms, underneath him. The hum of the engines firing vibrated through the soles of his boots. If Cyra had managed to get Jarn off Kolben, he might let her live.

Soon. His love would be back in his arms soon.

CHAPTER 9

Cifer glanced toward his cell door. A moment later, the wriggly pup—who seemed to have grown—pounced forward, held back by the big gray security male, Dez. "Mind if we visit?"

"Could use the company." Cifer sat up.

Dez opened the door, and Princess bounded in, raced to Cifer, and sniffed him all over. Cifer wrestled the pup off his lap, then his bed, and then off his lap again.

"She seems to think you have something for her."

Cifer shrugged. "I may have given her a treat the first time we met."

"Ah, that explains it." Dez pointed at the empty half of the bunk with a questioning expression.

"Have a seat." Cifer hoped the unsettled concern that flowed through him didn't show on the outside.

Dez remained quiet, and the low hum of the air recirculators filled the space. "How's it going with helping Blaize?"

"Good." Wasn't it? "I mean, I think it's good. I was able to help her reattach the lighting ballast and with a couple other tasks." Was Dez there to end the arrangement? Did Blaize not feel comfortable enough to tell him?

"Captain asked me to visit. Make sure you understood the trust Blaize is giving you by letting you help her in the most sensitive areas of the ship."

"Blaize and the captain have nothing to worry about. I'm happy to have some activity. And to be honest, it's a lot easier for me not to be in hiding the entire trip." Even though technically he still wasn't in his true form.

"Before this arrangement, when Blaize was bringing things to you here, she mentioned that you had a lot of knowledge of the ship. May have even been getting out of the cell."

Cifer stroked the back of his neck. How could he explain without lying? "I did a bit of roaming before I was discovered. But once I agreed to be held in the cell, I haven't...escaped." True, he never completely left the cell, although he may have *stretched* the boundaries. "I would never hurt anyone on the ship. I'm not violent. I don't contract for violence. I do contract to recover items. Sometimes items of dubious provenance or by dubious means, I'll admit."

Dez nodded and sat silent for a moment. He glanced up at the grate over the bathing alcove where the orb Cifer had stashed to keep from handling it too much glowed a soft-pink radiance. "Tell me about this."

"I don't know much."

Dez waited.

Cifer understood the silence game, even used it. But in this case, he was not on equal footing. "There was a contract put out by the royal family of Hiargus."

"Don't know much about that planet."

"Never been there myself, but I hear it's a nice place, natural resources aplenty. But they tend to spend more time investing in other planets, keep to themselves." Cifer was speaking from research. He hadn't been there yet.

"Pretty far from Kolben."

"What isn't?" Cifer laughed, but Dez stayed quiet. "This orb that I'm transporting, they use it somehow in their royal marriage ceremonies. Some wayward prince got his hands on it and tried to sell it, but he got picked up for other bad behavior and accepted a sentence on Kolben. Not sure he fully comprehended the situation. I have to get the little shiny ball back home in time for the next royal wedding, or all hell will break loose. Theoretically."

Dez narrowed his eyes and glared at the grate.

"In fact, besides paying for my transportation to Cassan, I'd like to discuss contracting *The Treasure* to take me Hiargus."

"Seems like overkill to book a ship this large for such a long trip."

"The length of the trip is what makes the ship compelling. Not sure where else I'd find a ship with a greenhouse and a chef."

"Chef?" Dez laughed. "Hardly. Just a better cook than anyone else on board. Believe me."

"How did *you* end up on Kolben? I understand there was a contract to deliver you? I mean, why would you ever leave Din' Gale?" Another planet Cifer had only researched but been intrigued by.

"Kolben wasn't my original destination when I left home. I lived on Baxianous with the man who bought my lifetime servitude. His heirs sold the contract." Dez crossed his arms, his missing hand noticeable. "The purchasers contracted Cyra to deliver me."

"And you two stuck to that plan?" It was obvious they were partners, lovers.

"She's honorable. As am I." Dez gave Cifer a pointed look that didn't quite land. Cifer was honorable as well, within his own code of conduct, which admittedly had some gray areas.

"Are you planning to settle down on Din' Gale now that you're not bound to the Kolben contract?"

Dez chuckled. "My mate is committed to her ship and her crew. And I am committed to her."

What would that be like? To have a person you would sacrifice your life and family for? Cifer would never know personally, since he had no family left to sacrifice for. At least, none he could ever return to.

"What about you?" Dez nudged Cifer, tearing him away from what would have been a series of dark thoughts. "Your people? Or planet?"

Cifer considered using his standard blow-off answer about the Universe could only handle one of his species. But Dez had been honest with him. "My planet of origin is on the far side of the galaxy. At one time, a wormhole connected it to the rest of the NOAH planets, but that no longer exists."

"You can't do a long journey? We went to Kolben from Din' Gale without using the ER bridges."

Cifer smothered his lost-child emotions. "Sadly, no ship capable of that particular journey exists. Even if I could find or build one, it would require cryogenics to make the trip without the bridge."

Dez nodded. "That's expensive."

"Very. Even the old NOAH ships can't make those long distances anymore. The solar arrays are too degraded, and no one wants to manufacture them. And that assumes there would be sufficient solar energy to capture, and I'm not sure there would be."

"Morgual—a planet near Din' Gale—had processing plants for the recycling of old cells. Pretty toxic remnants in the frames alone, and the cells, once they degrade, aren't really viable again."

Cifer nodded.

"It's funny. The NOAH ships were designed with the most advanced technology of their time. But no one considered the long-term impact of sending that—well, junk isn't the right word, but..."

"Most of the ships connected to make the core for Cassan."

"Hard to use solar panels with a distant sun. Could have settled the orbit closer to one or more of the solar systems, but they didn't have any idea which planets would be successfully terraformed."

"Unintended consequences. Morgual wouldn't be quite the disgusting planet it is if they didn't try to recycle or reuse those panels."

"But if NOAH hadn't used those panels, you and I wouldn't be here."

Cifer tilted his head and considered. "It's possible life would have formed on these planets anyway."

"A thing observed is a thing changed. Hawthorne effect."

"What's the solution?" Cifer asked. "Avoidance?"

Dez shrugged. "Patience and acceptance. There's no avoiding the fact that your actions, even the mere act of observation, can have consequences you didn't intend."

Was Dez hinting at an effect from Cifer's observation of Blaize?

"The best you can do is dampen the effect by taking considered action rather than reacting without a goal in mind." Dez sat quietly after his say.

Cifer wasn't sure if he agreed with Dez or not. So much of his life had required responding to the unexpected. The unintended consequences of someone else's actions. Did the method really matter, as long as he achieved the outcome he required?

After another few moments, Dez stood and went to the door of the cell. "Take care with her."

Did Dez mean "take care" to make sure they didn't form a strong attachment? Cifer had no intention of hurting Blaize physically or emotionally, but he wasn't ready to give up his life.

Cifer was still replaying his conversation with Dez when Blaize appeared. Her beauty took his breath every single time. Another reason he should keep their attachment as colleagues or at most friends—his appearance, his true self, did not make females gaze on him with desire. His current form was more useful, but what would be the point of starting a relationship or finding a life partner with whom he couldn't be his true self?

Better to stay disconnected and avoid heartbreak or other unintended consequences. She was too fine a person on every level to hurt in any way.

"Feel like stretching your legs?"

If she had any idea how far he could stretch... "Sure. What's on the agenda for today?"

His cell door opened, and she stood back. "Cable spot checks. I want to visually inspect every line we have. Usually, we'd do that in port on Cassan, but Cyra has other deliveries, so we won't be there long enough. Figured we could start now, and with two people working together, we might have a chance of getting through most of the visual inspection before we land, and I can order anything we need. I know crawling around in tight spaces and getting dirty isn't really appealing, but..."

Tight spaces and getting dirty with her actually sounded quite appealing. He grinned as he followed her through a corridor toward the crew quarters. She continued to explain her plan, and he let the melody of her voice flow over him.

"Sound okay?"

"Perfect." He grinned with his lips closed to hide his teeth. "Where shall we start?"

She selected a tool from her kit, bent down, and opened a

floor panel. Cifer appreciated the way her coveralls caressed her hips. She glanced up at him. "Ready?"

More than. "Yep."

She dropped her legs into the hole, sitting on the edge.

Cifer sensed a hesitation. "Want me to go first?"

She bit her lip. "No, I've got it."

Cifer prepped to follow as she shimmied into the maintenance space. It was about half a human high and maybe the same width. Tubes and color-coded wires ran in tidy conduits. Cifer shifted closer to Blaize, whose breath was shallow and rapid. "What are we looking for?"

With a shake of her head, she met his gaze. "Anything out of place, any signs of wear, especially around the turns. There should be adequate slack to avoid tension, but no sagging. That could indicate a problem somewhere up or down the line, or deterioration in the material itself."

Cifer was sure that Blaize wasn't comfortable with small spaces. He'd do what he could to ease her discomfort. He leaned a bit closer, letting his shoulder graze hers. "Do we want to work together or take different directions?"

"Together, I think." She flinched. "So we don't miss anything." With a deep breath, she shifted to her knees and crawled forward, neck craned as she visually inspected the veins of the ship. Cifer followed, reminding himself to check the wires and tubes, but he was primarily focused on the beauty in front of him. He was here to keep her from panicking in the space or get her out if she did. He couldn't think of a more delightful way to spend the day than cozied up to the hot redhead and protecting her delectable ass. Even temporarily.

"Does this look right to you?"

They'd been crawling through ductwork for what seemed like hours. Cifer dragged his gaze from Blaize and sidled closer, taking the opportunity to brush against her as he inspected the area she pointed to. She shivered, and he indulged in the vibration. The temptation to discover how else he might make her shake was irresistible—almost.

"Do you see it?" She pointed.

A slight—very slight—bulge in one of the tubes caught his eye. He would have missed it if she hadn't pointed it out. "Small bubble," he agreed.

She shifted and sat back on her haunches before digging into the kit she'd been pushing ahead of her. First, she snapped a picture. Then she dropped a pin on the digital map she had of the ship on her data pad. Finally, she wrapped the weakened area with some kind of reinforced tape. "That should hold until we get to Cassan. Have to replace that section before we head out again."

"How often do you do this?"

She blushed, and her pink cheeks were perfectly adorable. "I should have finished the inspection when I first joined on. But after the spiders escaped—"

"That explains the webs." Cifer craned his neck to peer down the duct they'd climbed through.

"First delivery for me on this ship. Venomous spiders."

"Venomous?" Cifer's skin rippled, and he struggled to maintain his form.

"I haven't been able to come down here since, even though I know it's not possible for any of them to still be on board. We counted the inventory when we delivered, and even if the count was off, after spending so many cycles on Kolben, anything in this part of the ship would surely have been dead by now."

Surely. Somehow that word didn't comfort him as much as it probably should have.

"Thank you for coming with me. Sorry I failed to mention the spider thing."

Cifer swallowed down his irrational fear. "Not to worry, Beauty. I'm happy to be your protector."

She grimaced, but it seemed more to hide her smile than any irritation with his words. "We're almost done. A few more meters, and we should be back where we started."

"Good thing you have the map. I'd be hopelessly lost by now." It was a white lie. He was aware of exactly where they were in the ship, but she deserved the praise for tracking their progress so well, braving her fears, and being so diligent with the care of the ship. He'd be sure to mention that as a reason he wanted to contract passage to Hiargus.

It had nothing to do with extending his proximity to Blaize. There was no future for them.

She was clearly dedicated to her job, as was he, but that meant traveling in different directions. And even if it didn't, there was no way he could maintain this form forever.

But there was nothing wrong with securing a safe, mostly comfortable ride to meet the obligations of his contract. As a paying customer, he'd likely be afforded a berth of some kind. A berth where he could relax his defenses periodically and possibly pursue a brief affair with Blaize. She deserved to know exactly how beautiful and smart she really was. If he did have a fling, it wouldn't be for selfish reasons at all.

Well, maybe a little selfish.

"Done."

Cifer snapped back to reality, away from the engrossing fantasy of Blaize naked in his bed. He followed her lush form through the hole. She secured the floor panel. "Anything else?"

She licked her lips, and Cifer would have given the balance in his credit account to know what had passed through her mind. She shook her head. "We're done for today."

"Then I'll see myself back to my cell."

"I'll go with you. I need to ask Veda something."

He grazed her elbow with the tips of his fingers. "After you."

Cifer placed his hands under his head and relaxed on the bed in his cell. He'd taken plenty of time to clean up properly, and after he was sure there were no stray cobwebs or spider legs anywhere on his person, he'd let his mind drift to the activities he would have preferred to spend hours engaged in with Blaize. Her writhing above him, begging below him, exploding around him.

His recently emptied cock twitched when her voice floated through the grate. He stood and stretched to hear her better, but Veda's voice came through next.

"You aren't even the least bit attracted?" she asked.

Blaize didn't reply. At least not that he could hear.

"You must know he's smitten with you."

"Smitten. That's such an old-fashioned word, Veda." Blaize's laugh made Cifer arch into the sensation of being caressed.

"You saved his life when we took the vote."

Cifer nodded to no one, but he'd listened in on that conversation too.

"Doesn't mean I'm attracted to him."

Cifer flinched.

"I've seen you working together. He can't take his eyes off you. Takes every opportunity to touch you."

He could remove the vent cover and see her reaction with his own eyes, but he'd bet that she was blushing, her cheeks attempting to match the gorgeous color of her hair.

"You're ridiculous. It's convenient for me to have a helping hand, and it helps him earn his travel. That's all."

"Running away from me won't change the truth," Veda said, her voice raised.

Cifer dropped back onto his bunk. Blaize came rushing toward the exit of the cargo area.

He called out to her. "My feelings are hurt, Beauty."

She halted. "What?" Slowly, she shifted back to his cell to face him. "What did I do?"

He rolled on his bunk, propped his head on his fist. Her gaze traveled over his mostly bare body. The briefs he wore left little to the imagination. The little wrinkle between her red eyebrows delighted him. He dragged a hand slowly over his bare chest above his heart. "You don't like me?"

"I—" She glanced over her shoulder toward the greenhouse. "How did you overhear our conversation? There's no way you could have."

"Actually, the acoustics in this cell are quite good. Like parabolics. What have I done besides help you?" He rose and slowly closed the distance between them, his gaze locked on hers. "I've been nothing but helpful."

"You're hiding something." Her breathy voice lit across his skin. He suppressed the shuddering urge to reveal himself to her. A pink glow flowed from the cell, making her even more tempting.

He gripped the bars and leaned forward. "But you voted to save my life."

She glared and brought her mouth closer to his. "Not because of any personal attraction. I saved you because I'm a good person."

He licked her words from his lips slowly. "Give me a chance." One moment alone with her naked, and he would prove to her. "I could be very, *very* good."

Her breath hitched, and her pulse raced along her neck. Heat from her body met his. She closed her eyes. Cifer prepared to meet her lips. She stepped back and marched away. The thud of her feet was nearly as fast and intense as his heartbeat. The pinkish light in his cell dimmed, and he dismissed the hollow ache that settled in his chest. She was a wicked temptation. Best he could offer was a brief interlude of intense pleasure. Better for both of them that she walked away.

Absolutely.

No question.

He angled his head, desperate for a final glance, but she was already beyond his sight.

CHAPTER 10

Blaize darted out the door and nearly collided with Veda, who was holding a meal tray. "Sorry, Veda." Blaize stepped around her to clear the entry. How had Veda gone from the greenhouse to the galley without her noticing?

"Are you okay?" Veda moved the tray to one arm and touched Blaize's forehead. "You look flushed. Was it the kiss?" Veda's cheeks darkened slightly.

"Kiss? I didn't—" Blaize glanced back. She and Cifer had been so close, Veda believed she'd been making out with him. "It wasn't what it looked like."

"I'm going to leave this with Cifer. It would be so much easier if he could join us for meals like everyone else instead of having to cart trays back and forth. I'll meet you in the galley."

"Good. I'll clean up first. Still have dirt on my hands." More than soap, she needed space. Time to clarify her thinking before she was around the others. If she started babbling in front of them, there was no telling what would come out of her mouth.

"Don't be too long. Dez has everything ready."

Blaize moved swiftly down the corridor to her quarters. Some cold water and a change of uniform, and she would be back to her normal controlled self, if she could figure out a way to forget the images of Cifer's mostly naked body. Her brain had no problem removing his shorts and filling in the blank.

Cold water. Too bad she didn't have time for a shower.

She took her usual seat at the metal table in the galley. There was seating for sixteen, but by silent agreement, the crew occupied the same half of the table at every meal, except for the occasions when Rhysa and Bodi were really battling. Dez sat to Cyra's left, close to the cooking devices. Veda always sat to her right. Rhysa sat next to Dez, which didn't seem to bother Cyra, despite the fact that the Blaque Poll female was a total flirt and couldn't keep her pink eyes to herself. When Blaize considered the situation carefully, it was obvious that Cyra had nothing to worry about. Dez was devoted to her. Rhysa enjoyed flirting. She couldn't help it. It would be like Blaize trying to make herself quit tinkering.

Had Rhysa been spending time with Cifer? She glared across the table at her.

"What?" Rhysa asked her.

Bodi took the seat next to Blaize. Dez filled serving platters, and Veda wordlessly placed each one on the table. The last meal of the cycle was the only meal they ever ate like this. Dez said it reminded him of home and was the proper way to share a meal. Blaize was thankful for the activity that distracted Rhysa from the confrontation. Rhysa loved arguing almost as much as flirting.

"What the heck *were* you doing to Cifer?" Veda asked her after the food had been served and everyone had started eating.

Blaize nearly choked. "Nothing. Why?"

"When I brought him his tray, he was breathless and kind of sweaty. You looked flushed when I saw you. I know you said you didn't kiss him, but is something going on?"

Had Veda seen Cifer with only the tiny shorts and the start

of an erection? The urge to tear out Veda's eyes rushed through Blaize before she could shake free. "So, you saw him with just his briefs on?"

"He was dressed." Veda smiled over her shoulder, almost a smirk. "He must have been undressed just for you."

"I don't know what you're talking about. The only thing going on is him helping me with the system maintenance. He's good with his hands."

Rhysa snickered loudly.

"I mean, he's talented."

Rhysa went from snickering to laughing out loud.

"With fixing things. Mechanical things. Sheesh. Get your mind out of the sex club." Blaize filled her mouth with food before she said anything else stupid.

Rhysa wiped away a tear. "I need to spend time with this guy. He has two of the most sexually repressed females I've ever met fighting over him. If neither of you want to keep him entertained at night, maybe I should."

"No." Blaize would give anything to take back that loudly blurted single word. She dropped her fork, her appetite gone. A few more cycles, and they would be back on Cassan, and this would be a bad memory. "Captain?" Blaize addressed the only sane woman at the table. "We found a small area in the water circulation system that should be replaced. Well, it's a small weakness, a bulge—"

"It so disappointing when the bulge is small," Rhysa interrupted.

"There's nothing small about his bulge. I mean—" Heat flooded her system. "The distention in the pipe—"

"Ooh. Distended pipes are my favorite." Rhysa fluttered her lashes over her pink eyes.

Blaize rolled hers and pressed her lips together. Nothing she said was right.

"Give her a break," Cyra told Rhysa. "Blaize. Are we in any danger?"

"No. It's a system check I should have done on Cassan before we left, but I got spooked by the spiders. Cifer went with me. I—*We* caught the issue early."

She'd admitted she couldn't do her job without help.

"That was smart. I had no idea you planned to inspect the ducts. Definitely not a job that should be done solo."

Blaize tilted her head. Not the response she'd expected.

"I appreciate the care you've taken with our engine and all our life-support systems," Cyra added. "Can we order the replacement part now, so it'll be waiting for you?"

Blaize nodded, not trusting her voice. Cyra was happy with the work. A weight lifted off her chest.

"If you get the information to me, I'll be happy to help with the order," Bodi said.

Blaize acknowledged the offer with a smile and nod.

"My captain?" Dez filled the silence with his deep voice. Cyra stroked his arm and gazed at him. "Our stowaway has become more of a crew member, and he's planning to not only pay for his transportation from Kolben but would like to contract transportation to Hiargus."

Cyra's face showed no surprise, as if they were staging this conversation for the benefit of the crew. "You believe he's no longer a security risk?"

"Correct."

Cyra glanced around the table. "Has anyone had a different experience?"

"Nope," Rhysa replied.

Bodi shook her head the tiniest bit.

"Can we please at least invite him to meals so we don't have to keep carting trays back and forth?" Veda leaned back in her seat and crossed her arms. "Anyone who objects can take over that chore."

Blaize gaped at Veda. She never spoke so adamantly.

Dez chuckled.

"I think that makes sense." Cyra smiled at Veda. "We should spend a bit more time with him before we commit to an extended trip. How far is Hiargus, anyway?"

"Depends." Rhysa pointed at Cyra with her fork. "Wormholes or no wormholes?"

"Plot it both ways, but we'll probably have to use them." Cyra sighed.

"I'll have answers by next cycle." Rhysa scraped up the last of her meal and filled her mouth.

Thank goodness the woman had something to focus on besides making Blaize blush.

"Why does he need to go all the way to Hiargus? What's there?"

"He's returning a stolen item," Dez answered.

"What is it?" Rhysa leaned forward, eyes wide.

"An orb owned by the Hiargus royalty."

"If he's having meals with us and is a paying guest, he should get his own quarters." Blaize regretted the words the moment she spoke them, but it was only right.

"A room next to yours, or are you sharing?" Rhysa grinned at her.

Blaize bit her tongue before she requested a room as far from Rhysa as possible.

"Dez will handle the room assignment, but yes, he should have a room instead of the cage in the cargo bay," Cyra acknowledged.

The rest of the meal was mostly silent. Veda and Bodi had clean-up duty.

"I'll see to our guest." Dez left the galley.

Cyra followed but went in the opposite direction toward the deck. Rhysa hadn't taken her eyes from Blaize, probably betting she would follow Dez. The temptation clawed at her, but she followed Cyra. Blaize could occupy herself with getting the part ordered and other tasks and hopefully overhear Dez's decision on the room assignment when he told Cyra.

Footsteps echoed in the hallway. Cifer launched himself to the door of the cell, anticipating Blaize. Instead, a pissed-off, dark-skinned, bald security officer stormed through the door.

"Furcifer Msuya. We have a problem." Dez's voice was harsh, but he wasn't nearly as scary looking as he had been the first time Cifer met him. Cifer relaxed back on the sleeping platform and flipped his sculpture in his hand. The piece was becoming a bird as he'd guessed, but he needed a few more parts. "What's the problem?"

"May I see that?" Dez came into the cell and held out his hand.

Cifer considered denying the request, but it wouldn't help his case. He sat up and placed his tiny creation in the male's wide outstretch palm.

Dez turned it about, inspecting it closely. "Very clever." He tested the tiny wings that could flap.

Cifer didn't take the trinket back. "Can you be more specific about what problem you have?"

"You were in the ductwork of the ship."

"With Blaize, at her request."

"She said you were very helpful. Not sure how you fit down there." Dez eyed Cifer.

His current form was closer to Dez in size. "I'm flexible."

"Hmm."

"As I said before, I am willing to pay for this leg of my journey." Cifer took the bird from Dez's still outstretched hand. He patted the empty side of the mattress.

Dez took the invitation and sat down. "Are you comfortable here in this cell?"

Cifer considered where Dez could be going with this line of questioning. "Beats any place I found on Kolben."

Dez laughed. "Very true. I stayed in this cell for a time."

"You did?"

"Yeah. Loud and drafty..."

"Again, not the worst place I've rested my head."

"The captain feels it would be best to have you join us for meals in the galley so that the crew can get to know you before they commit to taking you all the way to Hiargus."

"Hot food is a great incentive to face them."

"Face them?" Dez's forehead wrinkled all the way to his bald head.

"Five females who were not happy to have me on their ship?" Cifer shivered dramatically.

"You seem to have won two of them over already."

"Veda is very kind." Cifer rubbed his neck. "Blaize is..." So many words. Beautiful, brilliant, beguiling. "Uncertain of me."

"Blaize is very precise and careful with all she commits to."

Tightness hit Cifer between the shoulders. Her commitment wasn't his goal. He swallowed. "Wise."

"Why this ship? It's big and expensive."

"As I said before, the food is a big selling point—delicious despite being lukewarm by the time it makes its way here. And there's the care Blaize takes with the maintenance. It's hard to find a ship this safe." Cifer held out his hands and shrugged.

"Food is not reason enough to book an expensive, slow-moving ship for a long-distance voyage to deliver a ceremonial object."

"No, not by itself." Cifer stayed quiet. He didn't want to talk himself out of a ride, but he didn't want to tell Dez that not having to move the orb was a big motivator, along with more time with Blaize.

"If we were to consider taking you to Hiargus, the fee would be calculated from Kolben. We would need to charge for the return to Cassan from Hiargus if we can't secure another contract."

Dez wouldn't be able to come up with a number that was higher than the value of his contract to retrieve the orb. Add to that the value of spending time with Blaize, which was incalculable, and he would pay any price named.

Dez threw out a number half of what Cifer had been expecting. He winced by training. "Oof."

"You would join the crew in the galley for meals and have your own quarters."

"Now? Or do I have to wait until I can transfer credits on Cassan?"

"We have quarters available now."

"What about access to the data systems?"

"No."

"I'll bring my own data system for the leg to Hiargus. I couldn't risk having any tech with me on Kolben. But I have a business to run."

Dez frowned.

"A legitimate business." Cifer crossed his arms. Retrieving a stolen item didn't make him a thief. Technically.

"That will depend on the approval of the communications officer, Bodi, and Blaize, who will want to inspect your device."

"No problem. How long will the layover be at Cassan?"

"Typically, a few cycles." Dez stretched his feet out in front of him and crossed his hands over his stomach. "Blaize has the pipe repair to perform, and we all need time apart. Enjoy a few meals I haven't cooked."

Cifer chuckled.

"Blaize will do another thorough system check. Rhysa will want to negotiate with our fuel supplier."

"I have some business I need to attend as well." Cifer fidgeted with the sculpture and waited.

"Is there a time limit on your contract? We might not be able to meet it. This ship isn't built for speed."

Not the question Cifer had expected. "There is, but it's generous enough not to worry. I was able to acquire the orb faster than expected."

Dez nodded.

"Do you want the entire fee up front?" It was something he would never offer, but he knew once paid, Dez would be honor bound to deliver.

"I'll let the captain decide." Dez rose from the platform.

Cifer stood and held out his hand to shake.

Dez took and shook it firmly. "I'll be back once we have your quarters prepared."

Cifer relaxed onto his bunk. He had transportation to Hiargus and more time with Blaize.

CHAPTER 11

Varik's ship shuddered as it exited the wormhole. He shook off the lingering effects. "Scan."

"Yes, Captain." Karnek wobbled a bit in his chair and placed his hands on the built-in data pad. He clicked at the keys and glanced between two viewscreens. "No significant time loss." The displays zoomed out and in. "Captain, there's a very large ship directly between us and Cassan."

"Identity?" Varik's heart raced. It had to be—

"*The Treasure.*"

Varik glared at the blob on the screen. An impulse to blow it up shot through him, but he quickly muted it. His lover was on that ship. First, he'd rescue Jarn. Then he'd blow that ship, its crew, and especially the so-called captain into space dust. One step at a time. "Open communications."

Karnek tapped away, glanced over his shoulder, and tapped some more. "Not close enough."

Varek growled in frustration. "Get us closer."

"On it."

Varik gripped the arms of his captain's chair. His smaller ship, although not built for speed, should be able to close the gap. Each moment was an eternity. He was so close. Once they negotiated for Jarn, Varik would have his revenge. Maybe not on the Cassan space station, but Cyra would pay as soon as she left.

"Status."

"We're almost there, Captain."

Varik paced the bridge, no longer able to remain still. The urge to do something, anything, swamped him. Bend Karnek over the communication deck and fuck his ass until he got them in range. A visual of the man's toothy smile killed that idea, but Varik had to do something with the excess energy. Punch walls. Kick something. But he was the captain. And he didn't have another ship. Or another crew member. He'd take it out on Jarn for leaving him. For not getting back to the ship before Varik had to leave. Stupid boy.

And then traveling with Cyra on *The Treasure*—Jarn's ass would pay for that betrayal. As soon as he got him back.

"In range, Captain. What should I say?"

"Demand to speak with Captain Cyra about the male she is illegally transporting."

Karnek tapped away. He pushed a single button with finality and leaned back in the chair, arms crossed. "Now we wait."

Red washed over Varik's vision. A ping from the unit saved Karnek.

"No."

"What?" Varik yelled.

Karnek gave him a panicked look. "That's what they said. 'No.'"

"Tell them we will fire on their ship if they don't agree to release the male they took from Kolben."

Cyra wanted to play games? She had no idea what he was capable of. He'd blow up her ship, collect the space debris, and sell it to recyclers. He'd tell her parents she was working as a whore on the 3F station and make them search for her. He'd… he'd… He didn't know what he'd do if they didn't return Jarn, but it would be destruction on a level that would make history. He paced, tempted to tell Karnek to send another message, but what else could he threaten?

Maybe tell Cassan that *The Treasure* was carrying dangerous contraband? "What did they say?"

"Nothing."

"What do you mean, nothing?"

"They haven't responded, Captain."

Varik narrowed his eyes at the viewscreen as if he could blast the ship with his gaze alone. If only. Because the shitty scientific research vessel he'd acquired had no offensive weapons and minimal defenses. "Close in."

"Captain?"

"I want the nose of our ship up their ass." Cyra better know he meant business. "Also, tell them we're contacting the authorities on Cassan about the fact they're trafficking in sentient beings." There was no possible way they had any identification papers on Jarn. He'd left everything he owned on *Cain's Alibi*. Jarn would confirm Varik's story if questioned.

The Treasure loomed large on the viewscreen. "That's as close as I can get without putting us at risk."

Varik balled his fist.

"Do you really want me to send a message to Cassan?"

He was working with an idiot. "We have a ship with falsified papers, and they could be looking for our old ship ID if Kolben contacted them about our unauthorized departure. What do you think?"

Varik pressed his fist to his lips. No weapons. No safe way to interact with station security. The only advantage he had over *The Treasure* was speed. That might not be enough if

Cyra contacted Cassan first. Would she think of it? Even if she did, what could she report without exposing herself?

She'd kidnapped Jarn.

She was in the wrong.

"Wait. We got a message." Karnek stared at the screen. He glanced back at Varik, panic in his gaze.

"Read. It."

CHAPTER 12

Blaize's heart raced. Varik was back. Angry and threatening. His ship was practically in the cargo bay. If the crazy asshole rammed them... The ship had security settings, and it would lock down, but they could still die.

"Incoming message, Captain," Bodi called out.

Cyra halted mid-pace. "Read it."

"Captain Varik demands to speak to Cyra about the male she is illegally transporting from Kolben."

Cyra turned to Dez. "Bring Cifer—"

"On it, my captain." Dez spun on his heel and jogged off the bridge.

Blaize envied Cyra's ability to burn off the anxiety with pacing, but it would be a disaster waiting to happen to have both of them stomping around the bridge.

"What should I reply, Captain?" Bodi craned her neck to track the captain, keeping her hands on the keys.

"No."

"What?" Bodi's wings flickered.

Cyra froze, her hands went to her hips. "Tell them no."

Bodi tapped two keys, glanced back at the captain, and then clicked a single key to send the reply. Her gaze locked onto the screen. After almost no time, she flinched. "They say they're going to fire on us if we don't release the male we took from Kolben."

"How the hell do they know we took anyone from Kolben? We didn't even know." Rhysa threw her hands up.

"They're bluffing," Bodi said calmly and faced the captain.

"How could you be sure of that?" Cyra asked.

"That class of ship doesn't have the ability to fire on anything. My family owned several of them for short journeys to nearby planets. They're basically small transports with minimal amenities and barely any defense shields. That's why we got rid of them."

Dez returned with Cifer. Veda followed closely.

Cyra's gills flapped as she faced Cifer. "How do you know Varik Pectori?"

"Who?" Cifer's face screwed itself into a question.

"He's asking—no, demanding—I release you to him." She crossed her arms. "I want to know how you know him. How he knew you were on my ship when I didn't even know when we left Kolben."

Cifer shook his head and held up his hand. "Please read me what this Varik character has said."

Bodi read back the messages.

"He didn't use my name. He could be demanding the release of a person who isn't me."

"Possible," Veda responded. Cyra scowled at her. Veda shrugged. "Varik didn't use Cifer's name. He could be lying or confused."

"I don't know anyone named Varik Pectoral."

"Pectori." Cyra glared at Cifer. "How would he know we have anyone on board?"

"I filed our docking request with Cassan a couple cycles

ago." Bodi's wings fluttered. "It requires me to list the number of sentient and non-sentient beings on board."

Standard procedure. Blaize had filed those requests herself when she'd owned her own ship. When Varik had been her partner. She shuddered.

"He can't really fire on us. All bluster." Rhysa returned her focus to her screen.

"Are you sure?" Cifer asked. Bodi rattled off the details of the class of ship Varik flew. An image of the ship threatening them appeared on screen. Cifer shifted closer to the display. "That's not right."

"What?" Blaize asked.

"There was a ship on Kolben. And I paid for passage off the planet. They didn't ask any questions, but I didn't meet the captain. It left without me. It's the right size, but look at the name. He changed it." Cifer closed his eyes. "The *Harlan Johnson*. The identification number is different too, I'll bet. Stolen?"

"I wouldn't put anything past Varik. He still believes he should own *The Treasure*." Cyra moved behind Bodi, staring at the screen. "Is it possible he changed the identification chip too?"

"Easily," Cifer answered.

Blaize crossed her arms. She was torn between admiration and distrust. Cifer's knowledge of the possibilities for stealing an entire ship gave her a bit of concern. But his confidence, his calm in a potentially deadly situation, soothed her.

"If he left without you and you paid him, maybe he really is trying to get you back on board." Blaize didn't believe Varik would have any qualms about taking Cifer's credits and leaving him, but something didn't make sense. "He hasn't asked for you by name. Did you give him your name? Why would he be so committed to getting you on board? Where did you contract him to take you?"

Cifer's gaze never left her and he didn't interrupt, letting her finish. After she hadn't spoken for a moment, he replied, "I never met with the captain of the ship I contracted. And I paid to go to Cassan. We're nearly there. He wouldn't care to find me. Has no reason to."

Dez pointed at the ship on the screen. "More likely he thinks we have the person he tasked with blowing up *The Treasure*. Varik might be trying to keep the male from testifying against him if we file charges."

"If I were leading this negotiation," Cifer said to Cyra, "I would remind them if they harm the ship, the person they're looking for would be harmed too."

Dez moved behind Cyra. "But they aren't a threat."

"And if he went to the effort to change the identification, it's possible he retrofitted offensive weapons. We have to act as if his threat is credible."

Cifer had a point. Blaize squinted at the image, searching for signs of any modifications.

"Send the message," Cyra told Bodi.

Bodi keyed in Cifer's words. "We're nearly close enough to Cassan to be picked up by their sensors. They should detect the fake ID chip or at least send security since they're threatening us."

"Keep him engaged." Cifer pointed at the screen. "I'm not sure the authorities will see the ship as a threat, depending on what, if any, weapons they have. You could alert them, but as close as he is, he'd likely pick up the transmission as well."

"New message," Bodi announced. "He says we've kidnapped his crew member, and he's going to file charges on Cassan against Cyra Maejzur and Blaize Dreheer and everyone else on the ship conspiring in the crime."

"Ask him if this is the same crew member who tried to blow up my ship." Cyra's gills were moving fast enough to flutter her hair.

Scant moments passed.

"He responded that false allegations won't protect you from charges. He's demanding proof of life. A current image." Bodi turned to Cifer.

"Technically, we could...*fake* an image." He laughed. "But that would only make him more aggressive. We should try to defuse the situation or escape it."

Blaize stared at Cifer. How could he find any humor in the situation?

"Are you okay?" Cifer moved behind her and placed his hand on her shoulder.

Blaize swallowed the story about how she'd once trusted Varik that threatened to burst from her lips. There wasn't time. "We wouldn't be in this position if you hadn't snuck on board."

Cifer dropped his hand, and she regretted her attack immediately. Her past with Varik wasn't Cifer's fault. Nor was the current situation. She opened her mouth to apologize, suddenly at a loss for words.

"Blaize?" Cyra's voice yanked Blaize away. "Can we get a speed burst? Bump us into the Cassan sensor range and away from Varik so we can land first?"

"Yes, Captain." There were multiple ways to get a quick thrust. Since she didn't have to worry about burning fuel because they could reload their EMF rods on Cassan, her options were nearly limitless. She logged into the engineering systems.

Cifer moved closer to Bodi.

Blaize couldn't help the flare of jealousy that pumped through her veins.

"We need to string him along," Cifer said. "Ask what he wants as proof that the image of the bomber is current."

Bodi laughed. "He's not going to go for that."

Cifer tilted his head. "Never know. Oh, and tell him the person on your ship says Varik owes him."

Cyra snorted. "Now he definitely won't reply."

Blaize let her fingers fly over the keys, sending commands to the engine system. "Strap in."

Veda, Cyra, and Dez dropped into their usual chairs. Bodi and Rhysa grabbed their harnesses and clicked them in place. Cifer's head swiveled and finally settled on an empty station to Blaize's right.

"Hurry," she said.

He leaped and cleared the space in one go, dropping perfectly into the chair. Blaize gawped at him. She'd known he was flexible, but the jumping thing was new. Again, she didn't know this male well enough to be as attracted to him as she was. She closed her eyes and gripped the arms of her chair. The micro-burst of speed was over almost as quickly as it had begun. She softened in her chair, letting her body return to normal.

"Gross," Cyra said. "That was nearly as awful as a bridge crossing."

Dez rose and went to the captain.

"Sorry about that," Blaize replied.

"We're in live communication range of Cassan," Bodi announced.

"Good. Let them know we have an unknown ship following us and ask for early docking. I'm going to my tank." Cyra left the bridge without a second glance. Dez followed closely behind.

Fingertips grazed Blaize's cheek, sweeping her hair back. "Are you okay?"

She turned to face Cifer, wishing his touch didn't feel so comforting after the assault to her system.

"*Fuck.* That was awesome. I had no idea this ship was capable of that kind of speed." Rhysa grinned. "Better than sex. Almost."

Veda laughed.

"We could test that theory." The statement licked at Blaize's ear and dissipated to nothing. She blinked. Had she heard Cifer correctly? He'd already moved back to Bodi.

"Any response?" Veda asked what all of them were likely wondering.

Bodi tapped on the keys in front of her. "Nothing."

That didn't mean Varik was done harassing them. Blaize freed herself from the harness. That asshole didn't give up so easily.

Cifer followed her from the bridge. "What now, Beauty?"

"I have to check on the engines. The burst was not without risk to the systems."

"Where you go, I go." He matched her pace down the corridor.

His words wrapped around her heart like they were the truth. Her brain rattled with possible future scenarios of Cifer and her. She couldn't turn it off until she had something else to focus on, like her engines. No matter how fast she moved, he remained right with her.

CHAPTER 13

Cassan was Blaize's adopted home. Where she'd gone when she'd left behind the judgmental bullies on her home planet. A touch of nostalgia and security settled over her as she watched through the viewscreens on the bridge as the ship maneuvered into place and the bay sealed behind them.

Rhysa was the first to unbuckle. She stood and stretched.

"Don't run off," Cyra said as she freed herself. "We were thinking of hosting a celebratory meal tonight since we survived Kolben and Varik." Dez moved behind Cyra, her ever-present shadow with muscles. "Cifer, we'd be happy to have you as our guest."

"That's very kind of you." Cifer tucked his casual shirt deeper into the waistband of his pants. "But I have several items of business to attend to before we leave again, including transferring credits for the trip here."

Wait. What happened to *where she went, he would follow?*

"Of course. But if you change your mind or finish early, we'll be at the Sage Compound. Join us if you can," Cyra replied.

"Thank you," Cifer said and then left the bridge.

Blaize couldn't help but track him as he moved, graceful

despite his size. She rose from her chair and decided following him was a very good idea. It had to be something urgent and personal if he was running off alone. Despite the fact that she shouldn't care so much, she couldn't help it. "I have to check on a couple things as well, Captain. I'll meet you there. If I run late, start without me. I shouldn't be too long, but I'm not sure. I haven't spoken to the girls in the engineering program, and I'm supposed to have—"

"I'm in," Rhysa cut ub, and for once Blaize appreciated the interruption. "I'll see about our fuel first, though." A seductive purr laced Rhysa's words. She did a few side stretches and lunges.

Blaize would never see what Rhysa found appealing about Gareth, the hairy block of a male who supplied fuel rods. Except for the discounted price he charged them, which was more than attractive.

Bodi and Veda agreed to join Cyra and Dez as well.

Blaize left the bridge as calmly as she could. As soon as the ramp was down, she'd tail Cifer and find out what he was up to. Despite the sexual tension between them, or maybe because of it, she still had questions about him. Everything she'd seen had been honorable, but there were so many unknowns. Like why she couldn't keep her hands or eyes off him. Why she had an irresistible need to know where he was going.

Blaize hurried down the loading dock. Cifer had nearly cleared the bay, entering a crowded public area of the station. She raced through the bay, catching sight of him by intuition more than any particular characteristic. The dock was packed with the crews from hundreds of ships that landed and left constantly. Beings of every color, shape, and size swirled in a tight dance, intent on reaching their destination, while avoiding the hired sleds, the pedaled trykes for short rides, or the single person jet-scoots. Blaize hated those things. They had been an unnecessary danger to the rest of the inhabitants until there were rules against them. She scowled as one blasted past, nearly clipping her. Bits of conversations in universal Galaxian fell around her like confetti, mixed with other unknown languages, some punctuated with clicks, pops, and grunts.

Cifer moved quickly, driving forward with an uncommon grace. Bigger than most of the beings around him, he seemed to flow like water through the swirling morass, unfazed by the intense kaleidoscope of lit signs, loud sounds, and unidentifiable smells. Where could he be headed so urgently? If she found out he had a lover...

Nothing.

She would do nothing. But the idea of it made her hurry a little faster while she chastised herself about unfairly suspecting him. The entire point of following him was to gain more insight into who he was. She was so focused on not losing him, she bumped into a Gordinian. He released a cloud of gas designed to repel a threat that had her choking down the vomit that rose in her throat. No apology would appease a Gordinian, so she ducked away and moved faster.

She scanned the crowd.

Shit. He was gone.

Her gaze was drawn to the gold and red entrance of a fancy cafe she was somewhat familiar with, Pan Mandu, in time to see Cifer disappear through the door. Blaize slowed and let a few moments pass before she edged her way to peek in through the open screens.

A server led Cifer to one of the white cloth–covered tables toward the back with a woman Blaize recognized. She blinked and leaned back from the screen. What was *he* doing with Niquola Glinchart?

Blaize pressed her face to the clear barrier, her chest tight and breath rapid. He smiled at the stylish woman—the same smile Blaize had grown familiar with. The perfect turn of his lips made him appear charming and approachable. His focus was solely on the orphanage director, and he barely nodded to the waiter setting ice blue water in crystal tumblers at their places.

The director laughed and chatted with him like they had known each other forever. Blaize would give her right tit to know what they were saying, but there wasn't a chance in hell that she'd be seated in a swank cave like this. Her boots were a bit oily from climbing through the engine room before they landed. Her hair hadn't been brushed since she'd dragged a comb though it upon waking, hours ago. The beings dining in this place were polished and coifed to perfection. Cifer was especially handsome in a casual suit, his hair pulled back into a low queue. A stowaway, and yet he had a change of clothes? Time to fix his hair? That hadn't been what he'd been wearing when he left the ship, she was sure of it. Confusion wrinkled her brow as she replayed his path to the restaurant.

"Move along."

Blaize startled. The security officer had snuck up on her.

"Um, I..." Blaize needed to stay to see if.... What? If Cifer did one of his magic tricks for Niquola? If he touched her? If they kissed? Blaize shook her head. She was pathetic.

"Do you have a reservation?" The officer's sarcasm slapped the back of her head with its intensity.

"I don't." She couldn't lie. "I know some people in there, and I need to see what they're doing. I won't be a bother. I'm not a criminal. I know the woman. She's a good person. He could be trying to take advantage of her." Even as she made the lame accusation, she didn't believe it. "So really, if anything, you should be talking to him." Blaize bit her tongue, hard.

The words that came out of her mouth were gibberish, they erupted so quickly. She took a deep breath and peered in through the screen one last time just as the director reached for Cifer's hand. A strange stabbing pain tore through Blaize's lower abdomen, and she nearly doubled over.

"You need to leave."

The officer's voice broke her fall down the voyeuristic tunnel she'd tripped into. Blaize could visit Director Glinchart later in her office and find out more about Cifer. That was the point of following him—not stalking, not jealousy, and certainly not getting arrested, but finding out everything she could about who he really was before they began the next leg of their journey. For now, she would hole up in the minuscule housing unit she leased, clean up, and get some rest in a place that didn't require her constant attention.

"Blaize, it so nice to see you." Niquola Glinchart rose from her utilitarian chair and held out her hand over the plain metal desk with a warm smile plastered on her face. She wore the same navy skirt suit from earlier, her blond, nearly white hair still in its perfect updo. "I didn't know you were back on the station."

"It feels like I was gone for years." Blaize shook the woman's hand, the same one that had touched Cifer.

"Please, sit. Tell me about your travels."

Blaize gave her a brief summary of the planets they'd visited, leaving out a lot of details. She was here to get information, not expose her own emotional mess.

"Sounds like you've been busy, but what an amazing job."

Blaize basked in the approval from the woman she greatly admired. "I love it."

"The students in the academy seem to enjoy it as well."

"Really?" Blaize's chest lifted, filled with a warm glow.

"That's wonderful news. When you let me start it, I wasn't sure. I mean, not all girls feel about engines and systems like I do. But I'd hoped."

Niquola nodded. "It's the academy with the fewest absences and the longest waitlist. We've only had one drop out."

"Who?" Blaize had met all the girls in the class.

"Elaya." The director shook her head. "She fell in with some unsavories. We tried to talk her into coming back, but she couldn't be persuaded." The director straightened and smiled. "But we need to focus on the girls who are committed. We have a small class who will complete the training by the end of the galactic year."

"Excellent." Blaize swallowed hard. The plan for the academy had come together easily. But for the next level—working on live systems as apprentices—she hadn't made the progress she'd intended.

"We do have one apprenticeship spot. Voyagetech is willing to hire on one of the graduates as a junior tech full-time. We are using that as a reward for our top graduate. I have two females who are vying for it and working their tails off—one of them literally." The director chuckled at her own joke.

"I... That's great. I don't have anything else lined up," Blaize confessed. "But I can make some inquiries while I'm on station. I thought I would have...well, it doesn't matter what I thought." She'd thought she'd still be captain of her own ship. "It didn't work out. But don't worry. I'll line up more opportunities. It's the next step. My job has just been more intense than I expected. It's an older ship with unique design features, and I never expected to go as far as Kolben. Since I'm here, I'll make some inquiries, because as the plan stands now, I'll be going to Hiargus. And that's nearly as long a journey as Kolben, especially because our captain is not fond of ER bridges. We'll likely have to take at least one. And now that she has her mate, she seems…" Blaize stopped herself before she started rattling on about Cyra's love life.

"You know, I met with another sponsor who's been traveling. He might have some connections or be willing to sponsor an internship. He's very active with the organization."

Was she talking about Cifer? "That would be great. Who is this sponsor?"

"I need to talk to him first, but I think he would be willing to meet with you to talk about the program. He's dedicated to seeing our charges safely through their transition to independence." The director clicked on the screen of her personal comp. "In fact, I'm supposed to meet with him shortly to review some repairs and improvements we need at the juvenile facility."

"I'd like to meet with our academy students while I'm on station if that would be possible." Blaize was embarrassed. Normally that would have been the first thing on her agenda. Instead, she'd been focused on Cifer.

"Do you have time to do a presentation? Nothing formal. Maybe an insight into the daily life of an engineer during long flights or special techniques for facilitating ER travel? I know they would be fascinated."

"I'd be happy to do that. Soon. I only have a few cycles on Cassan."

"I'll schedule it with the principal." Niquola tapped on her data pad.

"In the meantime, I'll reach out to my contacts to find additional jobs or internships." Maybe Rhysa would have some ideas.

"Blaize, I don't know what we would do without you. Thank you so much." The director reached out and patted her hand, exactly as she had done with Cifer. Maybe they weren't lovers. Their relationship shouldn't matter to Blaize, but it did. More than she was comfortable with.

She left the director's office and went across to a diner, facing the building. Cifer would be at the director's office later. Losing his trail because of the stupid security officer had been frustrating. If she learned more about him, she'd feel more comfortable about agreeing to take him to Hiargus on the ship she lived on. It was only about the next journey, not the fact that she was falling for him. Not at all.

She didn't have to wait long. Her beverage was being served when she glanced out the screen and saw Cifer exit an expensive hired sled and duck into the orphanage. If she hadn't been looking out the screen, she would have missed him, he moved so quickly.

Before Blaize could finish her drink, Cifer and Niquola came out of the offices and waited on the edge of the pedestrian platform. Blaize swiped her credit chip and ran to the exit. They got into the director's sled, being operated by one of the students probably in training as a professional hack. Blaize raced to the underground tram entrance, bolted down the stairs, and boarded the crowded vehicle that connected all the parts of the huge station. She arrived at the juvenile facility in time to see Cifer and Niquola clear security. With no authorization and no story, she couldn't go in. She looked around for a place to settle in where she could see them when they left.

Time dragged on. At this rate, she'd never make dinner with the crew. How long did it take to look at a home for little ones? It wasn't like they had a lot to say, not like the females she sponsored, who were interesting and curious and intelligent. They were touring a facility for children who couldn't even deal with their own bodily functions. Blaize pushed her weight to the left side and rotated her right ankle. If they didn't come out soon, she would have no choice but to leave; others were taking note of her presence.

Finally, the doors opened. The director left in her private sled. Alone. Cifer crossed the thoroughfare, darting between crowds of beings and dodging the occasional jet-scoot driver. He walked directly to where Blaize had hidden.

"You could have joined us for the tour." His teasing tone set her on edge.

Heat crept up her cheeks, and the roots of her hair tingled. "I'm not... I wasn't—"

"Following me? You were, and I'm flattered, but I would be happier if you would share a meal with me. My treat. We can talk about the orphanage and the plans you have for the Engineering Academy graduates."

"Director Glinchart told you about my sponsorship?"

"No, she told me she had a sponsor. And since you spent so much time in her office earlier, I put it together. By the way, you're terrible at shadowing. If you want to improve, I can give you some tips."

"I wasn't... Fine, I was. But I'm not that bad."

"Good thing you know how to make engines sing." He looped her arm through his. "Let me feed you."

Blaize paused, checking the time. There was no way she could join the captain, so she allowed herself to be pulled along by the male who made her skin tingle and fought her desire to press her body closer to his. The muscles of his arm were like power cables—firm, flexible, and capable. Blaize's fingers tingled with the temptation to trace the lines up his arms and stroke his chest.

Cifer paused in front of a small storefront framed in light-blue metal siding. "This place is great. I make sure to eat here whenever I can."

"The Blue Skewer?" She'd never heard of the sketchy-looking dive.

"Yeah. Meats from all over the galaxy. Nothing fabricated. The special changes, sometimes hourly, depending on what's available, but it's always delicious." Cifer pulled her into the space.

There were mismatched round tables covered in images of planets from nearby solar systems. The seating was just as varied to support those with extra height, appendages, or unique shapes. Bodi would love the low-back chairs that wouldn't interfere with her delicate wings.

Blaize let Cifer order the special and two house brews while she inspected the artwork that covered the walls from floor to ceiling. It was primitive. White line drawings that were almost graphical on the dark, rusty metal siding depicted animals of all sizes and humanoid figures with long pointy sticks. One image showed the people holding the beasts at the end of their spears over a pit.

"They're ancient cave drawing reproductions from NOAH's origin planet, Earth." Cifer pulled her attention from the walls and back to the man who was as dangerous to her heart as the line people were to the drawn beasts.

"It's surprising that something so simple as a line drawing can be so dramatic, and the story is told so clearly."

"It's the essence, without all the layers that obscure the truth." Cifer was focused on the table and his voice was low.

"Exactly." Blaize took a breath to continue to discuss the artwork but was interrupted by the food being delivered to their table.

Blaize brought the first bite to her mouth and froze under Cifer's intense gaze.

"Eat. I want to see your first reaction."

She put the morsel in her mouth and moaned. Flavors

erupted on her tongue that she'd never tasted before, a perfect symphony of sweet and savory, spicy and tangy, with a hint of fire. She savored the bite and finally swallowed.

Cifer nodded. "I knew it. I knew you would appreciate this."

"How did you find this place?"

Cifer was silent for a moment and took a bite of the unnamed dish himself. Blaize got the impression he was stalling. She couldn't imagine why. Maybe he'd found the restaurant while doing something wrong.

"One of the kids at the orphanage. He used to eat out of their dumpster. Said it was the best place, but he had to be careful because the older ones would beat him if they found him nearby."

Blaize dropped her fork, her appetite misplaced and her throat tight. "That's horrible. I mean, I know they all have sad stories, but eating out of a dumpster and having to fight for those scraps? It's disgusting what happens to the little ones when they have no one to care for them."

"It's not your fault." Cifer stroked her shoulder.

"It feels wrong to eat inside at a table when the children are suffering." She stared at her plate.

"What good does it do to make yourself suffer? It changes nothing. You have to take action, not restrict yourself."

"Is that why you were meeting with the director?"

"You know, you really are terrible at hiding." Cifer laughed once.

"I kept my distance. I stayed in the shadows. That's what you're supposed to do."

He took a lock of her hair in his and caressed it slowly with his thumb. "You would have to hide this mane to remain unseen, even in the crowds of Cassan." He dropped her hair and dragged his fingers down her wrist and across her fingers.

"This pale, alabaster skin is more luminescent when contrasted to the darkness of a shadow." He paused and stared into her eyes. "And I would feel you. Know you were near." He put his hand over his own heart. "No matter how well hidden."

Blaize froze. She couldn't breathe. The things he said, the way her body responded to his words was indescribable. It was beyond reason and beyond her control. She took a shuddering breath, forced herself to look away, and put a bite of food in her mouth. The flavor was still intense, but her brain was offline, and it didn't fully register.

They ate in silence, cleaning their plates when Blaize recalled the question she'd asked, but he hadn't answered. "You didn't say. Why were you meeting with Director Glinchart?"

Cifer tilted his head, and his brown eyes bored into hers. He sighed. "I do what I can to help the orphanage. Their mission is so important. I was meeting with her to find out how things were going and if they needed anything."

"You give them money?"

"As often as I can. And I spend time with the kids who are struggling."

"That's so sweet."

Red spots flashed over Cifer's skin, so fast she almost missed it. "How long have you known the director?"

"She was one of the first people I met when I came to Cassan. I was trying to rent a room, and the owner was giving me a hard time. She was at the complex visiting a girl who had recently aged out. Checking on her, even though that's not the director's responsibility once they leave. When she first saw me, she assumed I was underage. After I explained where I was from and that I had a place at the flight academy to study but needed a room for a couple of months until the dorms opened up, she vouched for me. We kept in touch." Blaize trailed off.

There was so much more she could say. But she wasn't ready to share that story.

"Your first time away from home. You got into the academy because of the training you got from your mentor. The one who gave you the meter we fixed. That's why you started the training for the girls, to honor your mentor." Cifer had a way of seeing into her like no one else ever had.

"When I lost him, well...It was like losing a father." She pushed down her tears with a sip of the brew. "The adolescent females who want to go into the tech field can apply for a spot. It's voluntary. My mentor made all the difference in my life."

Tears filled her eyes, but she refused to let them fall. Her mentor had meant everything to her while he was alive, but he'd left her with nothing on his death except an old meter reader and another hole in her heart.

"They're lucky to have you."

"I wish I could do more."

"I do too."

They finished the remarkable meal, and Cifer swiped his credit chip through the mini kiosk at the table and then stood. He held out his hand to Blaize.

She considered him for a moment and then put her hand in his, letting him guide her from the cafe without a word of explanation about where they were going and what would happen next.

CHAPTER 14

Varik hovered in the shadows as the crew left *The Treasure*. First off was a male who looked vaguely familiar. Someone who'd worked with the underground lord Corvus, possibly? What was he doing with the sanctimonious crew of *The Treasure*? A few moments later, Blaize appeared at the top of the ramp and glanced around. She locked onto the nameless male and hurried after him. Next, the creepy bird-boned chick with the yellow skin and pink eyes paused at the top of the ramp, adjusted her breasts, and then raced down and into the crowd.

Back in the day, Blaize had been an okay fuck, but nothing special. Certainly not good enough to continue as her partner once he got bored.

Partner.

The word ripped through Varik. Jarn wasn't on *The Treasure*. The dock request had specified five females and two males. Varik didn't care who the other female was. Cyra's gray guard would be the second male. A primal scream lodged in Varik's throat as his heart ripped in two. Jarn was dead.

His beautiful boy, filled with light, was gone.

Cyra still had her ship, her crew, and her male.

Varik had...a score to settle that had just increased dramatically.

The bomb had failed. Taking the ship when the previous captain had died had failed. He'd been too direct in his attempts. He could use a man on the inside. Someone with experience. He rushed to follow Blaize. The male whose name he couldn't recall might be the key to making Cyra pay. If he'd had any idea how much she would fuck up his life, he'd have ended her immediately and made it look like something she'd done to herself. Hindsight was always in perfect focus.

Blaize clomped along through the crowds. Varik laughed so hard when the Gordinian gassed her, he nearly gave himself away. Bitch deserved that and more. He settled into a dark corner, easily tracking Blaize, who had the same idea of watching the male. How he didn't know he was being followed by that clomping beast of a woman with her flaming hair was a fucking mystery. But if he didn't see *her*, no way the male would figure out Varik was following them both.

A whisper of a touch made Varik jump.

"Missed you." Elaya slithered up to him, her body undulating in seduction. She'd been in the engineering academy Blaize sponsored. Varik had recognized the little rebel when he found her in a bar shortly after he'd broken things off with Blaize. Elaya had been a nice distraction but a bit of a pest.

Varik raised his hand to push her away but hesitated. She had her uses. He slid his hand down her multi-colored strands of hair, gathering it in his fist. "Of course you did."

Her mouth opened, and her split tongue poked out against her red lips. His cock twitched.

"I'm busy." He glanced over the female's head. Luckily, Blaize was easy to see with that flaming hair of hers. "Meet me in an hour."

Elaya dragged her finger down Varik's chest beyond his waistband. "Usual place?"

"No." He rattled off the district and coordinates for his rented room. The one he'd shared with Jarn before acquiring his ship. He'd planned to upgrade when he returned to Cassan with Jarn, but there was no point. And the location, in a seedier district of the station, offered a layer of anonymity that could be useful.

She repeated the information with a noticeable lisp.

"Wait for me."

She shot him a wicked smile and turned. Varik smacked her ass and rushed to where Blaize had disappeared around a corner.

The chase had been short-lived. Varik left Blaize lingering outside the dumpling restaurant, unaware of the security that had keyed on her. He fiddled with the image he'd grabbed on his data pad of the male as he entered an eating establishment known for business deals. Once he cleaned the image, he sent it to Corvus and requested information on who he was because he'd fucked up one of Varik's jobs.

Nothing to do but wait. Varik made his way back to the rented room, picking up a few supplies on the way. His data pad pinged as he neared the room. Elaya lingered in front of his door. Perfect. He checked the screen. Corvus had replied with a name. *Cifer.*

"Hey," Elaya swished her hips. "You made it."

Varik nudged her out of the way and keyed in his code, making sure she didn't see it. He'd change it after she left to be sure. He held the door open for her and followed her in. He'd left Karnek on *Cain's Alibi*. The ship had passed inspection on the little used repair dock, with the help of a friendly worker and a few extra credits. But Varik couldn't risk someone getting curious or Cyra coming around. The small dock was in one of the oldest sections of the station, but one could never be too vigilant.

"Cozy." Elaya's voice brought Varik back to the moment.

He stashed his purchases in the food safe storage and turned to his entertainment. With a quick flick of the magnetic clasp on his coveralls, the clothing fell from his body.

"In a hurry?"

"My dick missed your mouth." He stroked his cock and leaned back against the wall. "Why don't you kiss it and make it feel better?"

She took two steps and dropped to her knees on the dark floor. She tilted her head and opened her mouth. Varik smacked her face with his erection, and she stuck out her tongue. The split tip curled up invitingly. Varik shoved himself deep in her wet hole, grabbing her hair and taking control.

"Fuck. You're a good little cocksucker, aren't you?"

She gagged and made noises of assent. Her muddy brown eyes were the same color as the floor. Varik wrapped his fingers in her hair and moved her the way he needed. She teased his balls with her tongue while he fucked her throat. The gag noises were for show—designed to please him—because she had no gag reflex he could find. He straightened from the wall, his balls tightening. He rocked his hips and fucked her harder, the ridges of her mouth adding the extra sensation to send him shooting his load with a bellow. She slurped up every drop and licked him clean.

He pulled free, and she ran the back of her hand across her mouth.

"Good girl." Fucking fantastic was more like it. Nearly better than Jarn's mouth. She had the kind of skills that could get a male to break to her will. A weaker man than him, but still.

She sat back on her heels and tilted her head, probably expecting something for her performance.

"Take off your clothes and play with your pussy. Make yourself come."

With a grin, she whipped off the scant dress. Naked as the first day she'd breathed, she parted her thighs and sucked her fingers into her mouth. Varik moved to the bed to sit. "Turn around and face me."

She lifted to her knees and twisted around.

Varik tossed her a pillow from behind him. "Put this under your ass."

With a few adjustments, she laid out on the floor, legs bent and parted and fingers in her pussy. "Fuck yourself, but don't come until I tell you."

Varik grinned when she immediately went to work, shoving her digits deep in her glistening hole. The slurp and sucking sounds were the perfect soundtrack to inspire him on how to get to Cifer. If Blaize was following him, the male mattered to her. Blaize held the engineering job on *The Treasure*. If he provided a little distraction, she'd screw up. Varik had catalogued her weaknesses long ago.

Moans disrupted the spiraling plans that hadn't quite come together. Varik rose and placed his foot on Elaya's throat. Bored his gaze into hers. Her movements became frantic. Fingers fucking. Hips bucking. Mouth open, unable to gasp. Captured and weak. But she didn't roll away. Didn't slap at his foot. Perfectly obedient. An idea snapped into place. He could use Elaya's assistance. She'd do exactly what he asked.

He lifted his foot. "Come."

CHAPTER 15

Blaize tried to keep up as Cifer moved faster and faster along the main causeways filled with beings and transports. Finally, it got to be too much; she was panting for air and jerked to a stop. "Where are you taking me, and why are you dragging me? I'm not a thuringy on a lead. I thought we were going for a walk, but you obviously have someplace in mind. And it's not that I won't go. I probably will, but you should talk to me, ask me."

"I'm sorry." Cifer dropped his head, and before he moved away, Blaize stepped into him and wrapped her arms around him. His solid strength was so in contrast to his soft words. "I want to... I was going to show you my...my rooms. Where I live. When I'm here." He closed his eyes.

"You're taking me home?" No one had ever willingly brought Blaize into their private space.

The attraction between them was undeniable and only increased when she was this close to him. But what did she really know about him? And what was he still hiding? Because she was certain there were secrets she still had to discover. But he was taking her to his home, his most personal, safe place. And were his secrets bigger than him saving her life from the falling ballast? More important than him protecting *The Treasure* from Varik? More indicative of his character than him providing for the orphans?

"Will you trust me?"

And that was the question. Blaize hadn't easily trusted anyone since Varik had devastated her entire life. But Cifer didn't control her livelihood, her safety, or her self-worth. If anything, he'd done more to protect and support her than anyone since her mother was alive. He was the one being vulnerable. With her. "Yes."

"It's not really a home." He held out his hand to her again, and they walked shoulder to shoulder. "It's nothing special. Too small to be called...anything. But I've rented the space for years."

A large male bumped into Blaize, knocking her back. Cifer seemed to expand in size, his copper skin taking on a redder hue, and he clacked his jaw. The inconsiderate male jumped and murmured an apology before racing off. Blaize doubted what she'd seen, because when she eyed Cifer again, he seemed exactly as he had been before, although his gaze was still locked on to the retreating guy. She tugged Cifer's hand, and he instantly focused on her.

"Are you okay?" He swept her hair back and caressed her jaw.

"I'm fine. It was nothing."

"It was rude. Nobody should touch you." He glanced down at their clasped hands. "Unless you want them to."

"I want you to." The words slipped out, and the glow inside her chest ratcheted up, along with the heat between her thighs. Cifer's grip tightened, and he tugged her forward, moving faster than before. Blaize grinned and raced to keep up, his urgency spilling into her.

The structure he paused in front of was an elongated

capsule that had been constructed when the quarters along the edges of the station had no longer been sufficient to house the growing population. Blaize had studied the construction of Cassan in her spare time while at the academy. The way it had come together so long ago, originally from the Earth ships reconnecting and then as manufacturing took hold. Cassan grew organically. As a result, it could never be used for travel again. Instead, it remained in place, its own jumbled planetoid.

He guided her onto the power lift, and they emerged on the sixth floor and walked a short way down a curved, dim hall to a gray door that looked like all the others. He keyed in an access code and turned the handle but didn't press forward. "I haven't been here in...too long."

"I'd like to see it." Desperately. The urge to push past him and inspect the hidden parts of him was overwhelming. She grazed her fingers down his arm. "Let me in?"

"You're the first one I've brought here." He wrapped his arm around her waist, pulling her close.

Blaize pressed her lips to his, and the hallway disappeared. There was only Cifer. His heat and taste, the tangle of his tongue with hers. A door slammed shut. She ended the kiss, her lips still tingling. They were in his room. She hadn't been aware of moving inside, she'd been so caught up in their kiss.

Blaize took a few steps forward, and the lights brightened with her movement. She gasped, trying to see everything at once and finally turning in a slow circle. "This is yours? You did all this?"

"Uh-huh." Cifer went to the tiny refrigeration unit. "Do you want a drink?"

"Cifer, this is... There aren't words." Statues like the small bird Cifer had made on *The Treasure* filled the walls and surfaces. Bins of parts were lined up on a small desk. He handed her a glass with cool water. She sipped it and moved toward an object that reminded her of a winged insect she'd seen pictures of once as a child. The long, segmented body was slightly longer than her fingers, and its gossamer wings jutted to the sides, changing color depending on the angle of her gaze. "How did you create the wings?"

"Scraps of a material that appears translucent. Very expensive stuff."

She dropped her hand to her side to keep from touching it and possibly harming the fragile material.

"Do you like them?" He lifted his hand and swished it through the air as if he could capture all of his creations in one swoop.

"Do I like them? Cifer, you're an artist and a mechanical genius. These all move, don't they? It's obvious they do—the articulations, the details. Do you sell them? Where did you learn to do this?"

"I just started making them when I had time on my hands."

"But how did you learn?" She picked up a tiny, half-finished bird from his desk. A light tap of her finger, and both wings flapped several times before coming to rest. "The movement is so realistic."

"I just played with them until they did what I wanted." He shrugged and turned away.

"You should have been an engineer. I mean, assuming you aren't because you're a..." Heat rushed up her cheeks. "Sorry. I'm not sure what you call yourself." The word thief had nearly popped out.

"No apology needed. I do break the rules, frequently." He filled a second glass of water from the chiller and sipped it. "But just so you know, lately, even before I met you, I've been trying to get away from that world, or to at least do something good with my...talents."

"You're very talented. And you do a lot of good for the

orphans." She reached for a sculpture suspended from the ceiling. "What is this? It's not a bird."

"No, it was a creature on my home planet. Like a bird, but it lived in caves and came out at nightfall with all of its fellow creatures."

"It looks creepy."

"It's misunderstood."

"How are you not an engineer? You have the natural talent." Blaize couldn't make sense of everything she knew of him. She'd known he fiddled with the parts he found and made things. But the creations in this room were incredible. *He* was incredible. Blaize caressed his cheek. "What happened to you?"

He hesitated. Shrugged. The color of his skin shifted to a green tone and back so quickly, she almost missed it.

"You don't have to share," she said gently.

"I was young, maybe eight. I'd had a fight with some of the other kids. So, I was by myself when they took me."

"*Took* you?" Blaize's heart crumpled in her chest.

"Pirates. They'd heard about my people, and they wanted one of us. I was—" Cifer hissed out a breath. "Trained. Used. Kept against my will. I didn't get to complete my formal education or discover what else I might have been good at."

"But that's criminal. You could have them arrested. Why didn't you? Why didn't you go home? I mean, I assume you're not still working for them." She stepped back as the horror of his situation hit her and the possibility that he might still be trapped.

"No, I don't work for them any longer. I freed myself. But my skills are, let's say, *unusual* in polite society. And I can't go home. That option closed long before I was able to extricate myself."

Blaize warred with her urge to hold him and offer comfort, but the tilt of his chin and the steel in his spine didn't invite coddling. "I learned to defend myself young too. But I was lucky. At least for a while. I told you about my mentor. He was like a father to me. When he died, I was no longer allowed to work as an apprentice. When I lost him, I lost my vocation too. And for a long time, I lost my direction. Then my mother passed, and she left me some credits. I sold everything we had and came to Cassan for engineering school. I had to pass the entrance exams because I didn't have a formal education." An idea popped into her brain. "That's something you could do. You could pass the exams and go."

"You're fucking brilliant." He caressed her cheek, nudged her hair behind her ear. His gaze was an unspoken invitation, and she pressed against him. His solid body anchored her in a way she hadn't felt before but had longed for before she understood exactly what she searched for. He saw her. Beyond the red hair and the desperate talking. He saw *her*.

"I want to show you my bedroom." He sounded like he was choking on every word, struggling to make his demand a request.

She handed him the empty glass.

Cifer put the glass down on the few square centimeters of his workbench that wasn't occupied by his metal sculptures and took her hand in his. There was no hallway, just a door—one of two interior passages.

"It's not a palace."

"I live on a transport ship."

Cifer closed the small gap between them, bodies connecting and his gaze locking to hers. "You deserve a palace."

Blaize laughed. Her life was so far from royalty.

He palmed the door, and it slid into the wall with a faint scraping sound. With a tap of his hand, the ceiling panel illuminated enough to see without blinding her. She crossed into the room. The screen over the large oval portal, mimicking the shape of the building on its side, reflected their image. He nestled against her back. Her pale skin and red hair contrasted with his dark-brown hair and coppery skin. They looked like an abstract image of the place she'd been born. Coppery clay, fiery sun, crystal underground water. Home, but better.

Her eyes met his in the reflection briefly before she reddened and turned away. The room was the complete opposite of the rusty metallic main room. "It's so colorful in here."

The walls and ceiling were vivid blue, and the bedcover was a yellowish-green. For the first time, she wasn't the most garish part of a room.

"Will you stay?"

He wasn't just asking her to stay. He was asking for her to trust him. To be vulnerable with him. The last person she'd bared herself to betrayed her. Ruined her.

There was a good chance that Cifer would be a short-term lover. Someone she could be with while she rediscovered trust in herself and they traveled to Hiargus and back. Her future was on *The Treasure*. His future was unclear after the return trip. Although their time together might be short, it might be enough.

"Yes," she whispered, scared of her answer but not of him.

He wrapped himself around her and kissed her as if she were the last drink of water on a barren planet. He licked at her lips. She gripped his arms and opened her mouth to his. He had cared for her, fed her. She gave him what she could: her warmth, her passion, her desire. There was a chance she'd regret her choice, but at that moment, the only regret she could see was not staying. Not exploring the connection that had built between them. Each conversation when he'd listened without interrupting. Each time she discovered evidence that he was an amazingly good person who cared about the kids like she did. Each time he'd touched her like she was valuable.

She dug her fingers through his long dark hair and pulled him to her. As close as she was to his solid strength, it wasn't enough to satisfy or even cool her heat.

He broke their kiss. "Too many clothes."

She whined at the loss of his lips. At least he was panting. She whipped her shirt over her head. Cifer's gaze branded her with its intensity. She froze.

What was he thinking?

Too pale?

Were her boobs too big?

When she wasn't in shapeless coveralls, she wore loose shirts, ordered them a size larger than she needed. Maybe he didn't like big tits. She lifted her arms to cover her chest, but Cifer reached out, a blur of movement, and stopped her.

"Don't." His voice was thick and low. Stepping closer, he released her arms and trailed his fingers across her chest, below her neck but not touching her breasts. He lifted his gaze. "Who stole your fire?"

"Fire?"

"You *are* your name—Blaize—igniting desire so deep in me, setting me on fire. Yet, I see the doubts trace across your face." He caressed her cheek. "And I want to hurt whoever gave them to you." His fingers trailed lower. "So soft."

Emboldened by his desire, she released the clasp holding her bra closed and dropped her hand without parting the cups to free them. Cifer's eyes dilated in the low light, but the ring was white. Not pale like hers—white, with black lines radiating from the pupil. Those were the eyes she'd caught flashes of, but this time, they remained. He drew his hand down her chest and gripped one side of her bra and paused, asking her permission silently. She nodded, a tiny little movement that meant he could do what he wanted. With his other hand, he gripped the silky fabric, and he parted the panels to free her.

He didn't look—he kept his eyes locked on hers—but he caressed and stroked and gripped her flesh. Pressed his hands underneath and felt their weight. He teased her nipples with his fingers. Her buds tightened to hard points. He pinched them, and when she would have protested, he captured her mouth with his. His body pressed against hers. He still had his shirt on. She pulled the sides of the fabric, but the top didn't come loose. Cifer released her mouth and removed not only his shirt, but all of his clothes in a flash, setting them carefully on a low chest. They settled into a gray mass, looking nothing like what he'd been wearing. The oddity didn't hold her attention long because he stood before her, boldly naked.

The sight of him was magnificent.

There were more muscles on his arms and abdomen and legs than she'd ever seen on another humanoid. His warm copper skin seemed to almost shimmer, like it was luminous. He was stunning. When she finally let herself look at his cock, her heart raced, and she couldn't draw a breath.

There was no way. He was...thick.

And long.

Even his balls were big and heavy.

He'd break her with that thing.

But she wanted him. Wanted him to stretch her and ruin her. Leave her body used and aching. Instead of running, she toed off her boots and slid out of her pants, leaving her panties on as a last flare of panic hit her.

"You were made for me." Cifer spoke as if his thoughts had sneaked out. He gripped her hips in his hands and spun her so her back pressed to his chest. She could see them reflected in the screen, her ghostly pale skin, his shining brown warmth. His white eyes caught hers in the image. That's right. He hid too. She'd never seen his real eyes before that moment. He still had secrets.

He kissed her neck, licked the crease where it joined her shoulder, and suddenly, she didn't care if he was hiding something. She tilted her head, giving him more access to her skin.

He pushed the band of her panties down over her hips and let them skim down her long legs. She stepped out carefully, not wanting to fall. When she returned to their reflection, what she saw took her breath away. Cifer was pale, the exact shade of her skin. Where her head rested on his chest, he was deep red, identical to her hair. She blended perfectly. For the first time in her life, she didn't stand out like a warning light on a control panel. Tears filled her eyes. "You're so lucky. I'd give anything to be able to blend." She shuddered. "To belong."

"You can belong to me. Or I'll belong to you. I'm yours. If you want me. Even if you don't," he said softly in her hair.

Wordless, she turned and pressed him back to the brightly covered bed.

"Go back. I want to see *you*."

A brief frown crossed his face. His skin slowly took on the luminous copper shade she was familiar with but suspected was an illusion as much as the pale skin had been. She didn't care. He was hers. At least for this moment in time.

She straddled his hips, pressing his hard length between her wet lips of her pussy and his stomach. She rocked her hips once. Cifer groaned, and she couldn't hide her satisfied grin.

He narrowed his eyes. "You like that. Teasing me."

She smiled, a seductive grin that felt foreign. "I want to tease you and torment you and then take you inside and ride you until we both come undone. I want to please you. Make us forget the past and only be here. Now."

Cifer slid his hands up her thighs, holding her gently.

Blaize leaned forward and kissed him. He rose to meet her. She broke away, compelled to know every part of him. She traced her lips down his neck and over his chest with little nibbling kisses, noting where he shivered and where he jumped. He was ticklish in one tiny spot—right where his arm connected to his body. She nipped him tenderly before moving on. Every time she moved, kissing his nipples, licking them, her hips rocked, coating his cock in her desire.

"Please," Cifer begged, pain in his voice.

She lifted off his cock so she wouldn't hurt him, disappointed that her explorations were not complete.

"No," he called out when her pussy left him. He gripped her hips and flipped her underneath him.

Blaize was both relieved and frustrated. She wasn't sure how to take control during sex, but she wasn't done.

"I promise, you can do whatever you want to me, but let me have that sweet wet pussy first. I don't care how. You tell me. My fingers, my tongue, my cock? Whatever you want, but I need you. Please."

Blaize was unable to find her words with the visions he'd created of his hands and tongue and cock.

"What do you want? Anything."

"You. I want *you*. Inside me." She'd beg if that's what he required.

"This?" Cifer gripped his thick length and held it up to her like an offering, his eyebrows raised.

She nodded.

"It's yours, Beauty." He notched the swollen head at her wet entrance. "Protection?"

"I'm covered." She couldn't wait. She thrust up. They gasped in unison.

She was full, achingly full and stretched. As if his entire body filled every space in hers. More. She needed more. With a twitch of her hips, she tightened her grip on him. He groaned and shifted deeper, eliminating the last millimeter of space between them. He kissed her, his tongue between her lips, and she sucked it hard. Neither of them was moving. She tried to figure out how to take him deeper—into her soul. He felt like the place she belonged. Like there would never be a place in the universe that was better than where she was right now. And then he released her mouth, and his hips pulled back and he thrust into her, and it was even better.

Threads of light danced through her vision. It was like traveling through an ER bridge, her body being reformed and time becoming meaningless. She moved with him. His length slid in and out, hot and wet with her slick juices, overloading her systems. Every thrust she met increased the intensity of their connection, as if she welcomed him into every cell. She never wanted it to end. He was shaking in her embrace, his thrusts rougher and less rhythmic. She tried to keep up, but her body couldn't be controlled. Then everything was gone. She was a supernova, exploding, as if light erupted from every pore of her body.

She screamed. Cifer's deep voice joined her, and heat filled her. Consumed her. Left her panting for breath and boneless. Cifer collapsed over her and then rolled to the side, taking her with him, his solid length still embedded inside her, where he belonged.

He clung to her with one hand, his legs entwined with hers, and stroked her hair with his other hand. There were no words for what had happened. She'd had sex before. What they'd done wasn't sex; it was something else, something undefinable and unique.

"How did you do that?" The words fell out of her mouth, and she wasn't sure what she was asking.

"Do what?" His breath caressed her ear.

"Become me?"

"Ah, the skin."

She nodded against his chest.

"It's camouflage, at the cellular level. All the members of my clan have the ability. I suspect it was to aid in hunting when we were more primitive."

"It would be incredible to be able to blend anywhere."

"It is my greatest strength and the thing that has instigated the most pain."

Blaize couldn't imagine how blending in could have hurt him. "What do you mean?"

CHAPTER 16

Cifer hesitated. "I wouldn't have been kidnapped if I didn't have this...skin."

Blaize trailed her fingers up his torso, and it was all he could do to quickly camouflage the trails left from his reaction to her touch. Not that it mattered. She knew his secret.

At least part of it.

The other part he didn't share with anyone. Ever. Because if she saw his true form, she wouldn't want him at all. He wasn't stolen for his aesthetics; the pirates took him because they could use him.

Her exploration continued, waking every part of him. His body vibrated with need for her, which made no sense. He'd come undone earlier, experiencing an orgasm that tore through him with a force he didn't know he was capable of. But as long as she was near, he would want her.

He wrapped his arms around her and rolled her on top of him. Her hum of pleasure pulsed through him, her soft body molded to his, and he met her lips in a soft, slow kiss. She traced his face with her fingertips. He stroked his hands slowly down her back, along the curve of her amazing ass. He'd only had glimpses of her form under the work uniform she continually wore on the ship. When she'd shed her clothes, it was like a surprise present revealed. Exactly what he hadn't known was possible but was absolutely perfect. His cock stiffened between her thighs.

She wiggled around until the tip rested at her hot, wet opening.

Cifer groaned. "Don't tease me."

"I'm not. I'm savoring you." She rocked her hips, taunting him with her sweet pussy. "Too fast last time."

"Slow and easy, as you command."

She arched her back to gaze at him. "I don't think anyone commands you."

"You could."

She slid farther down his cock, and he moaned. Her body and his delayed gratification made for the most exquisite test of his patience—a gentle seduction as she took him deeper. She peppered kisses over his chest, his neck, even his ears, which had never been sensitive before but had become an erogenous zone. For her.

The silken slide of her skin overwhelmed his control. Without regard for where, he let his hands roam across every part of her body. He parted the soft globes of her ass, caressing the forbidden space. A small part of him concentrated on maintaining his illusion, because she could make him forget himself and completely let go. And that would be a disaster. But he couldn't resist the temptation of extending part of his authentic body to her sensitive opening. As soon as the tip of his tail connected, her pussy clenched and released another wave of excitement, but she stiffened.

Damn.

He retracted and reformed, still teasing and gripping but not testing. She hid her dark desire from him. It was only fair since he still hid from her. If she could have forever with her, he would come out of hiding and bring her out of her shell at the same time. But while he'd intended to figure out how to extend their time together, there was no forever. She was committed to *The Treasure*. And he was committed to the orphans.

For as long as they could have, he would hoard every moment, lock it away in his memories. Her movements up and down his cock intensified. He lifted his hips to meet her with each descent, seeking the depths of her, to memorize the experience of her owning his body.

She moaned and panted. He took over lifting her in his grip, taking their connection into the realm of the impossible. She held on to his forearms and gave up control.

"Touch yourself."

She released one arm, and her fingers went to the tiny center of pleasure that would detonate them out of orbit. Her pussy clenched around his cock.

His back arched, and his balls drew up hard. "Fuck," he roared. "Come. Do it."

Her fingers sped up, and he slammed deep into her channel and held her tight. Hot jets of cum erupted from his cock. Her sweet pussy answered with an ocean wave, and for a brief moment, he let himself float away.

She collapsed onto his chest, eyes closed, murmuring about how amazing and good it was. Thankfully, she was so lost in her own sensation, she wasn't aware that he'd lost control and his natural skin color had taken over. He quickly camouflaged and fought the urge to relax into his natural shape.

He slowed his breathing to match hers, his cock eventually softening and falling from her body. The parting twinged his heart. Her face was obscured by her hair, and he brushed it back to check her. Gorgeous...and asleep. Good.

"You're a good person, Blaize. I wish I could say the same. But I can't. I'm a bad guy and I don't deserve you, but I won't let you go until I have to." His words were soft. He didn't want to wake her, but the urge to be honest compelled his confession after connecting so deeply.

A chime sounded, and he carefully freed himself from Blaize's body. He'd rather stay in the room in her arms or at least admiring her, but no one came to his door by accident. He tugged on his discarded clothes and pulled the bedroom door almost closed behind him.

Cifer scowled at the person in the hallway. "What're you doing here? How did you find me?"

The young woman shrugged. Her multicolored hair was pulled back in a tie, and her dress was in need of a wash. "Wasn't easy. But you're the only who can help."

"With what?" The back of Cifer's neck prickled.

"There's a shipment coming in." She stepped closer. "Kids."

The instinctual clack of his jaw made the girl jump back. "From where?"

"All over. They've been recruiting from everywhere."

Cifer narrowed his eyes at the misuse of the word *recruiting*. But coming to Cassan with a ship full of kids didn't make any sense. How would they get past— Credits. Low-paid security people were easily bought.

He glanced over his shoulder toward the bedroom, but all was quiet. He could wake Blaize, but she'd want to help him. The unknowns made this far too dangerous a mission for someone with no experience and no ability to blend. He'd explain himself when he returned.

There was no way of knowing what time it was. The room was dark, but the screen was still in privacy mode, so the station's virtual sky illumination wouldn't come into the room even if it was daytime hours. Blaize rolled over, missing Cifer's heat. Voices had awoken her. Both were familiar, but they didn't belong together. The female who spoke had a distinctive lisp, a result of having her tongue split as a child. A crude punishment for lying in the house where she'd been sold. Elaya. The girl who had left the engineering academy, despite having two more years of eligibility. What was she doing at Cifer's?

Shipment of kids?

The front door snicked shut, and the voices were no longer audible. Blaize leaped from the bed and fell right back down. Damn, she was sore. First order of business—find the bathroom. Walking was a challenge, but she hobbled out of the bedroom and through the only other door in Cifer's place. It was utilitarian and white, but it did have a bathtub, which she eyed longingly. Unfortunately, there was no time. She peed, wincing as the liquid hit the areas that had been chafed. That done, she washed her hands. The muscles in her legs were starting to recover now that she was moving around. The ache inside only seemed to intensify, demanding more of him, but he'd left.

She hunted for her clothes. Her panties were nowhere to be found, but the rest she threw on. Maybe Cifer and the girl would still be on the other side of the door. A chime sounded. She rushed to the door, curious why Cifer wouldn't just let himself back in. Did he need help?

Varik filled the doorway. Blaize stepped back and tried to close the opening, but he grabbed her shirt and tugged her forward. "Where's Jarn?"

"Get your hands off me." She pushed at his chest but stumbled forward when he didn't let go.

"Jarn," Varik yelled in her face, spittle dotting her skin.

"I don't know who you're talking about."

He wrenched her into the hallway and slammed her

against the opposite wall. Cifer's door auto-closed. There'd be no getting back in. She rammed her knee between Varik's legs as hard as she could. His blue skin paled to nearly match hers. She wrenched her arm against his elbow, breaking his grip, and screamed, "Fire!"

As she ran down the curved hall, she smacked her hand against the doors, bellowing, "Fire!" over and over again. She didn't wait for the power lift. Instead, she headed for the stairs. As soon as she pressed open the door, an alarm sounded. Let Varik fight his way through the crowd.

With each stair, another question occurred to her. Why had Cifer left with Elaya? How had Varik found her?

She escaped the building and slapped her pocket, relieved to find her data pad where she'd left it. At least she could pay for transportation to take her back to the ship.

The Treasure looked the same when she exited the hired sled a few minutes later. As if time hadn't passed at all. She'd been gone for...hours? A cycle? But her world was completely different.

Different, but the same. She still hated Varik, more since he physically attacked her. She was still obsessed with Cifer, and he was the guy who'd left her in his bed to run off with a young woman—probably for a good reason, but it still hurt to be left behind.

Of course, the ship looked the same. She only wished things were different. She keyed in the security code and lowered the entrance ramp. The ship echoed in the way that only spaces devoid of life did. Everyone was likely still enjoying the dinner she'd skipped. Maybe she should have used that as an excuse to leave instead of jumping into bed with Cifer. There was no way to go back and change it. She closed herself off in her quarters, a space that felt more like home than her rented room. After stripping off her clothes, she took her time under the hot spray of the shower. Her body missed Cifer's touch. Her brain tried to imagine all the reasons he could have left that didn't have to do with her being inadequate. He was an excellent lover, but what if she wasn't?

And nothing explained why Varik had known where she was or even cared.

CHAPTER 17

"Wʜᴀᴛ ᴅᴏ ʏᴏᴜ ᴋɴᴏᴡ?" Cifer followed the spy down the hall. She'd given him tips in the past that had worked out but had never come to his rooms—shouldn't even know where they were.

"Cruiser landed in dock 141-XA—fast, newer."

Cifer focused on her lips to make sure he heard her clearly. Some words came through—mostly. Others were more challenging. "How long?"

"Hour. I pinged you."

He glanced at his data pad and noted the missed messages. He considered sending something to Blaize, but involving her in his business would only put her in danger. If anyone became aware of how much he cared about her... He hated the tug of duty and desire. Had avoided it with casual connections. But there was nothing casual about how he felt about Blaize. He'd been so deep with her, he'd almost shown her his true form. She'd understand why he left once he explained. She cared about the lost kids too. The stolen, the sold, the abandoned. "How many kids? Any idea how old?"

"I counted five. Young. Maybe as old as ten? I'm not sure.

But they all look different from each other, and they're in a cage."

At the word cage, Cifer saw red. He'd spent galactic years being locked up. Bastards had either stolen or purchased the young, both of which were against the Galaxian law. Not that those fuckers cared. It was all about the sale or keeping them and training them to commit crimes the adults couldn't pull off. They were in for a rude awakening. Cifer was on-station, and they weren't going to make money on that shipment. The only downside of having to take paying contracts was being away from the station. He had an older crew of former orphans who worked around the various sectors of Cassan and could fill in for him, and frequently had to, but there was nothing he liked more than seeing the stolen kids returned to their families.

He rushed after Elaya so that maybe he would be in time to get the kids. And maybe he could make it back before Blaize woke up.

Instead of a ship, as Cifer expected, Elaya stopped in front of the Rusty Bucket. A dive bar for space crews. He scowled as he stepped through the door.

"It's that guy. In the corner." Elaya pointed to a table in the far back.

Cifer should have known a Gordinian cum-stain was involved. He'd suspected as such, based on the descriptions from the previous kids who'd been saved. If he were a more violent being, he'd stab that fool through his black heart this very minute.

Cifer glanced around the bar. Elaya had slipped away. Smart girl.

He clacked his jaw at the gelatinous, hairy fuck as he

passed on his way to the restroom. Better not to shift his appearance in public too often, and he had no idea how many eyes were on him. Elaya was occasionally useful, but she delved into the dark allies of the station far too much to be fully trusted.

Once he'd adopted the persona he'd use to negotiate with child slaver scum, he slipped back into the bar, taller, leaner and the muted shade of forest fungus. He stopped in front of the table. "Elaya sent me."

The Gordinian kicked out a chair. "Have a seat."

Cifer crossed his arms. "I was told you have merchandise."

"You're not the only interested party."

"Why would you think I'm interested when I haven't seen the goods?"

The Gordinian laughed, and a belch of noxious gas wafted over to Cifer. "You'll see them soon enough."

"Soon enough would be now." Cifer made sure his voice clicked in the way of the species he mimicked.

"First, we have a drink."

If he did that, there'd be no way to return to Blaize before she realized he was gone. Cifer pulled out his data pad and sent a message to his most loyal operative. A kid who'd gone through the system and was as passionate about saving the young ones as Cifer. "This isn't a social event. I don't have time to sit around drinking with you. Either you have the goods, or you don't."

The Gordinian checked his data pad, not realizing the screen was reflected in the dirty mirror behind him. He tapped out a message. Not every word of the message was clear, but the recipient might as well have been lit up. Varik Pectori. Cifer took a calming breath. Their little game had become exponentially more interesting.

That was the captain who'd abandoned him on Kolben.

The one who had attacked *The Treasure*. Blaize would absolutely understand why he had to leave.

"Change of plans."

Cifer glared at the evil fuck.

"The other buyer is temporarily delayed."

"I'm not interested in playing games. I'm here now. The other buyer obviously isn't as invested as I am. Show me the merchandise." Despite Varik's involvement, Cifer's main concern was the kids' welfare.

"That's not how this works." The kidnapper named a time. "Meet back here."

The kids would be stuck in the cage for another cycle if his connections couldn't find the ship first. Elaya had been very specific. "I'll give you one more chance." Cifer had to stay in the dominant position for the negotiation. "Either we resolve this business, or I'll find another supplier. It's not like you're the only procurer of live goods."

He stood slowly, like he had all the time in the world, and left the noisy bar.

Cifer raced home. The word never applied before Blaize had been there. He made it back as fast as he could. The sheets were messy. He flipped them straight and found her abandoned panties, but she was gone. He wasn't surprised. Disappointed, but it was a minor setback for a very good reason. First, he had to make sure the kids were safe. Then he'd find his beauty and make amends. Even if she was angry, he had the whole trip to Hiargus to make it up to her.

A text came in on his pad.

No XA-141 in standard docks. Still checking auxiliary.

No surprise. Shady shit didn't happen at the main docks, but it was prudent to verify. He considered his options, and like a lightning strike, an idea came to him. A devil of a plan. If it came together.

"Cifer calling for Master." He nearly choked on the last word. But the minion answering the call would expect proper protocol, and he couldn't afford not to be received.

Time passed in silence. The man who demanded the title of Master might still be mad that Cifer had managed to escape. Master loved to play games of risk. Cifer had studied him for years before negotiating to win his freedom. It hadn't been a foolproof plan, but it had worked. No matter how much he hated the male for stealing him from his home, his influence was a useful tool on rare occasions. And once Master had abandoned the flesh trade for more lucrative endeavors, Cifer had reinitiated a basic connection. He hoped it wasn't broken.

Finally, background noise filled the connection.

"Cifer, my son. It has been too long since you called. Have you been well?"

The words made Cifer's stomach curdle. Master was no father figure.

"My apologies for being out of touch." He could have said more—made excuses about being on Kolben—but that would lead to more questions he didn't want to answer. Cifer went silent and waited. The minute of silence extended into an eternity. Another test. Eventually, he was rewarded.

"What's on your mind?" The male's voice was resigned, just like when Cifer had won his freedom.

"Varik Pectori. I recall he owed you a debt." It was a risk. Cifer had only heard rumors. But if Varik was indebted to Master in any way, then Cifer's plan might work. His blood raced as if he were running for his life.

"Why would you care?" The irritation in Master's voice barely covered his suspicion.

Cifer squelched his glee. "He has a meet set for twenty-one hundred. Apparently, he's dipping his toe in the flesh trade."

A growl filled the line before Master asked, "How is this my concern?"

"He's meeting the trader at the Rusty Bucket. Didn't know you allowed others to do business out of there." And the hook was set.

After a telltale pause, Master found his voice again. "Why inform me?"

"Varik broke a contract I prepaid." Cifer had written off the fees he'd paid Varik, but Master would believe money prompted his call. And Cifer had already set the pieces on the board by confirming Varik owed Master. Cifer's debt would transfer, too, in the old pirate's mind.

"Hmm. We should meet with Varik. You and I. Resolve this." If Varik could hear Master's voice right now, he'd piss himself.

"I'll be at the Rusty Bucket." He hung up without saying goodbye.

The call had gone better than expected. Not only would Varik be in a world of hurt, unable to negotiate his contract with the buyer, but the goods would be long gone when he shook himself loose of Master for the evening. And Cifer might get his money back. He'd need to play it cool so that Varik didn't suspect him of freeing the kids.

Blaize startled awake with Cifer's name on her lips. The drab walls of her quarters were a stark reminder that she wasn't in his bedroom as she'd dreamed. Irritated, she dressed in a fresh set of coveralls and stomped down the corridor to find her fellow crew members in the galley.

"Blaize." Veda smiled, a cup of tea in her hand.

"Are Dez and Cyra here?"

"Captain had some business to take care of. Dez wouldn't let her go alone. They took Princess with them." Rhysa inspected Blaize with narrowed pink-eyed.

"Do you know when they'll be back?" Blaize addressed Veda, hoping Rhysa would let her be.

Veda shrugged. "I made first meal. There's plenty, if you're hungry."

It would be awful, but she was starving. "Sure. Thanks, Veda."

Veda scooped a chunky, liquidy brown gruel into the bowl and placed it in front Blaize. The others already had theirs, but she waited for Veda to join them before they ate. The first bite confirmed that it was as disgusting as it looked, but she was hungry, so she took another bite and quickly swallowed.

"Where were you last night?" Rhysa asked with a teasing tone. "We missed you at dinner."

"Based on the fact that your face is as red as your hair, I'd say you had fun," Bodi added, teaming up with Rhysa at the worst time.

Blaize filled her mouth with glop. She didn't want to, but chewing would give her a valid excuse not to respond.

"It's none of our business." Veda sounded sad.

Was Veda attracted to Cifer? Had she hurt her friend? She would find out, but not in front of everyone. Even if Veda was attracted to Cifer, he wasn't a good male. He'd told her so when he thought she was sleeping. Blaize wasn't sure she believed him, but she would make sure the Veda understood she wasn't missing out on anything worthwhile—besides the best sex of Blaize's life. "I had some errands to take care of that took me longer than expected. I...I stayed with a friend."

"A male friend?" Rhysa wasn't going to let this go, so Blaize did something she hated. She lied.

"Nope." She dropped her spoon in her empty bowl. She

patted Veda's shoulder before she placed her bowl in the sterilizer. "Thanks for cooking." She couldn't bring herself to tell Veda it was good. One lie was enough.

"No problem." Veda reached out and grabbed her hand as she was leaving. "Can you help me?"

"Of course. What's wrong?"

"Well, I think I broke the lighting system. Nothing will turn on."

"I'll take a look now." Blaize was relieved to have something to focus on besides the mystery of Cifer and the attack from Varik. A technical problem to solve was exactly what she needed. She could have kissed Veda.

"You're not mad?" Veda was back to her bright, cheerful self. So, she wasn't interested in Cifer... She was worried Blaize would be angry about the lights.

Blaize laughed. "These systems are fragile, and not every ship has a grow room. Bound to be some technical issues. I'm surprised it's done so well. I mean, I put it together so it would last, but you know. It's a work in progress."

"Thanks," Veda called out behind Blaize.

She thumped down the hallway toward her beloved engineering systems that didn't run off, didn't claim to be bad, and didn't leave her aching with emptiness. Engineering systems were her first and last love. Cifer was just a blip.

CHAPTER 18

Blaize swiped the back of her hand across her forehead. The lighting problem had been tricky to track down, but finally she'd found the problem. Fixing it had involved some contortion and a whole lot of swearing, but the plants were back to basking in the faux sunlight. She tucked the tools away and headed for her quarters. The idea of a shower compelled her to move her tired, sore body faster than usual.

She met Veda in the main corridor. "Blaize. Did you figure it out?"

"I did. There was a crack in the insulation of the main wiring going into the room. I had to rerun a new length of wire and then test everything." Fuck, she was too tired to explain. "The lights are working. I left them on. Your timer should still work, but I don't know if you need to adjust the settings for the time your plants were in the dark. I'll leave that to you. I need to get this grime off me." She swept her hand down her body, showcasing the patches of filth smearing her coveralls.

"Thank you so much." Veda clapped her hands together. "Will you join us for last meal? Dez is cooking."

Eating in? When they were on Cassan? Not that Blaize

minded saving some credits. Also, she really should talk to Dez and Cyra about Cifer. "Sure. I'll be there shortly."

"No rush. He's just starting the prep." Veda flashed a smile and hurried off to her plants.

As Blaize showered, it occurred to her that almost the entire cycle had passed and Cifer hadn't shown up. Where the hell was he? It hurt that he hadn't come looking for her. It wasn't like she was hiding. The ship should have been the first place anyone looked.

Clearly, he wasn't. She sighed and scrubbed the soap from her hair. Stupid. Again. She shook off the regrets as she finished cleaning up and dressing. At least the last person she'd slept with wasn't Varik anymore.

"Blaize, how nice." Captain Cyra was seated at the galley table with Veda, Bodi, and Rhysa.

Blaize plopped into an empty chair between Veda and Rhysa, leaving the one next to Cyra for Dez.

"It's almost done." Dez didn't turn around. He was poised with a heat mitt over his remaining hand and eyes glued to a timer.

"It smells good, whatever it is. I can't wait to try it." Blaize tried to remember when she had last eaten. Maybe the crap breakfast Veda made and a couple of protein bars. At this point, Veda's cooking would probably taste appetizing.

"Thanks for getting the lights working again." Veda touched her shoulder gently. "What was the real issue?"

"Well, the power was being drawn from cells that charge while the ship is in motion. After we stopped, the cells weren't charging. I created a failover—well, not really a failover because it's not an automatic backup, but an alternate source for when we aren't in motion. You won't need it often, but it should be seamless. Next time we stop, we'll know for sure, although technically, I guess since it's working now, it's already proven."

Cyra chuckled. "I guess you've been busy."

Dez put a plate in front of the captain and then quickly served the rest of the crew. He didn't have to, but he said it made him feel good to take care of them that way. At first, Blaize had been uncomfortable. Instead of wrestling with the discomfort, she made sure to do nice things for Dez as often as she could so he would know she appreciated him.

"We'll be ready to go in two cycles." Cyra broke the silence of the focused eating.

"Two *more*?" Bodi's jerked her head up, eyes wide.

Dez joined them at the table. "There's been a delay offloading the Kolben equipment, and Captain and I found a place that will do some intensive training with Princess. We have to spend most of a cycle with her, learning the commands."

That made sense. Not a good idea to have a protective animal with no training or control. Princess had grown considerably since she was born. Still a cute puppy but definitely showing signs of what she would be like as an adult.

"Where to next?" Rhysa asked.

Cyra glanced at her mate with a soft smile. "A stop at Din' Gale to see Dez's parents."

"Oh. That will be wonderful." Veda smiled. No surprise their hobby gardener wanted to revisit the jungle planet.

"Then a quick stop on Chalcanth." Cyra almost swallowed the name of her own planet. "Then we head to Hiargus, as contracted."

Maybe. Only if Blaize failed to convince them to drop the contract with Cifer. That weird orb he'd brought on board was still in the vent over his former cell. The glow had caught her attention when she'd been working on the lighting issue.

"What're we doing on Chalcanth?" Rhysa asked.

"Visiting Cyra's family." Dez spoke in a tone that invited no further questioning from the inquisitive navigator.

"Well, then, we better go out tonight." Rhysa looked directly at Blaize.

"I have to..." Before she could finish her sentence, Rhysa was shaking her head.

"No. We're going. We need to have fun as a crew before we're locked in again, and you skipped out on the team dinner."

"I need to take care of something," Bodi argued with Rhysa as always.

"Do it later. We have two cycles. Tonight. Bar."

Blaize had seen her like this before. It would be easier to just go along. She'd talk to Captain Cyra and Dez before they went. "Fine, I'm in."

Veda put the fork down on her empty plate. "I'd like to go."

"Of course you're going." Rhysa tilted her head with a jerk.

"Cyra and I will remain here to watch over the ship now that the new fuel has been loaded." Dez's deep voice invited no argument, even from Rhysa.

Cyra blushed, turning a faint shade of lavender.

"You're out of excuses." Rhysa pointed to Bodi. "Unless, of course, you want to take us to your club?"

Bodi had a club? How did Rhysa know that?

"What?" Bodi was swiveling her head, looking at each of them. "I don't know what you're talking about, but I'll come tonight. For a little while."

Rhysa grinned hugely, having gotten her way. "That's fine. You don't have to share...yet."

Bodi stood and took her plate and Veda's to the sterilizer. "I'll be ready in two hours," she called over her shoulder as she strutted out of the galley.

Blaize wondered how a female learned to move like that. If

she tried to roll her hips like Bodi, she'd look like she needed to relieve herself.

"Be ready." Rhysa pointed a finger at Blaize. "No coveralls. Sexy clothes."

Blaize rolled her eyes. "Fine."

"I'll be ready too." Veda cleaned up her place and darted out.

As soon as Rhysa had cleared the doorway, Dez pinned Blaize with his yellow-eyed stare. "What do you want to talk about?"

How did he know she wanted to talk to them?

"You're usually the first one out with excuses about work."

He even answered her questions without her speaking them. She swallowed her doubts. "It's Cifer. I don't think... I'm not sure he's who he says he is. I think he might be up to something."

"Any evidence?"

Blaize tried to figure out a way to explain that he'd disappeared with Elaya and that Varik had been at his rooms. But every way she rearranged the facts, it still led to her admitting that she'd been in his rooms. She wasn't ready to confess she'd been intimate with Cifer. "I think he might be using the orphanage for nefarious reasons."

Dez gazed at her, unblinking.

Cyra asked, "What makes you think that?"

"I followed him after he left the ship and..." And saw nothing that would sound bad. *Shit.* She didn't like that he was going off with Elaya, but there was nothing criminal about it.

"I'll keep your concerns in mind. I'm glad you brought them to my attention."

Blaize stood. "Right. Okay."

Unless she uncovered something heinous in the next forty

hours, she would be traveling with Cifer to Hiargus for galactic months. Ugh.

The Rusty Bucket was packed with crew and other less savory characters, including the ones Cifer had asked to join him. He left Master and his goons in the shadows of the bar at a tall table and sidled around the room, not quite in camouflage, but less than obvious. Music pounded, and the center of the bar had become a makeshift dance floor for a few grinding beings. The Gordinian occupied the same low table in the far corner, facing the door. Varik strutted in, and Cifer took advantage of the distraction to adopt his persona and shift into the Gordinian's peripheral view.

The goon gasped with a stinky eruption. "Where the hell did you come from?"

Cifer lifted his lips in a predatory grin.

Varik neared the table and pointed at Cifer. "Who are you?"

"It's none of your business who I am." Cifer glared at Varik but addressed his question to the dirtbag. "Why are you letting this overgrown fish disrupt our business?"

Varik sputtered. "*Fish?* You rotting corpse of fetid fungus."

"I'm amazed they let your kind in this bar." Cifer held back a grin. Establishing dominance in the negotiation had been too easy.

The Gordinian raised his bulk from the chair. "Sit down, Yonash, before you draw the authorities."

Cifer, responding to his fake name, settled into a chair facing Varik across the small round table.

"So..." The word came out with a belch of gas. "Where shall we start the bidding?"

"On what?" Cifer asked.

"You know what," Varik insisted.

Cifer turned from Varik to the slave trader. "I haven't seen any proof you have the goods."

The slaver held up his data pad, the live streaming indicator on, an image of five children in a pile in a metal crate. As Elaya had told him, the oldest appeared to be about ten.

"They look dead." Cifer rolled his eyes as if he didn't care.

The Gordinian tapped a message on his pad and held it back out. An arm holding a rod shifted into view. Cifer stiffened. He'd been electrocuted more times than he could count with a similar device. The bar smacked the cage, and the oldest boy jerked awake. "Good enough?"

"Sure," Cifer said, swallowing the urge to kill the Gordian there in the bar. The location of the children was still unknown. He had to be patient.

"They're smaller than I expected." Varik sneered. "What are you hoping to get for them?"

Cifer kept his blank face firmly in place.

"This is quality merchandise." A noxious puff of gas accompanied the declaration.

Varik wrinkled his face and recoiled. "I need a drink."

Cifer glanced back at the bar to flag down a server and froze with his hand in the air. Flaming red hair caught his attention.

Blaize.

At the worst possible time and place.

CHAPTER 19

The Rusty Bucket wasn't packed, but it was still early. They secured a round table in a high booth tucked into a shadowed corner against the metal walls faux oxidized with the impression of rust. A server approached. His ill-fitting black tech pants, speckled with pockets, barely reached the end of his long, lean legs. Ankles with a large brown and white pattern peeked out. An unruly shock of blond and brown hair stood on end, as if he'd been electrocuted. Blaize wondered if he endured ridicule for his appearance too.

"Blue Crowns, all around," Rhysa announced.

The server loped off, and Rhysa gave the team a devilish grin. "We are queens, after all."

Bodi flinched. "Careful what you wish for. It's not as exciting as it sounds."

Rhysa placed her elbow on the table and rested her chin on her fist, locking her gaze on their communications expert. "Convince me."

Bodi's wings fluttered, and she searched for support. But Blaize was curious about Bodi's culture, and Veda seemed to be fascinated by the crowd.

Bodi opened and shut her mouth several times before she

was saved from answering when the server returned with their drinks.

As soon as each of them had a glass of the swirling, shimmering blue concoction, Rhysa raised her glass. "To queens and their *Treasure*."

They clinked glasses, and Blaize sipped the drink to be polite. An exotic, fruity, fizzy mouthful had her silently thanking Rhysa for ordering. "Delicious."

Rhysa laughed. "Of course it is."

"It's good." Veda set her drink on the table. "I suspect it might be strong."

"Anything you put in your mouth should be." Rhysa blinked her eyes in a flirty manner.

Bodi laughed. "Don't pretend you're that discerning."

Rhysa swept back her white-streaked brown hair with an almost golden hand. "Well, if it isn't strong, it better be tasty. This meets both criteria."

"Sure does." Blaize hoped they wouldn't get into a fight, but Bodi laughed again and took another sip. It was the most relaxed she'd seen their navigator in too long.

"Oh!" Blaize blurted the single syllable as it occurred to her that she could change the subject and get information from her partners. "I don't know if you know, but I work with an engineering academy for girls. Orphans who are aging out of the system. I help with the academy as much as I can. They teach all the skills for them to be techs or engineers on ships." Blaize paused. "Anyhow, the first class is moving toward graduation, and I told the director I'd look into internships, but I haven't had much time or luck. Do any of you have any ideas?" Blaize sipped her sparkly drink and waited.

"Really?" Rhysa's head bobbed as if she'd been struck. "I had no idea you did that or that the school existed. That's such a great idea. Although, I'm not sure I'd put any young women on the ships I've been on."

"Most of my contacts are back on Arbotriz," Bodi said. "But if they don't mind traveling, there might be some great opportunities, and ours is a female-centric culture. Less chance for abuse."

Rhysa nodded in approval. "I could ask Gareth if he knows of anything."

"Thank you. I wasn't sure how I would keep that promise. Even something on station, doing repairs or other tech work, would be great."

Rhysa nudged her. "I got you."

Sooner than was prudent, Blaize ordered another. The first one barely muted the running analysis on what Cifer was up to, why he'd left, why he hadn't come back, what she would do for the time they traveled to not only Hiargus, but the stops on Din' Gale and Chalcanth. Awkward wouldn't begin to capture her feelings if she had to avoid him that entire time. Maybe he'd found another ship. Maybe she was worried over nothing.

The bar filled with more crew from the nearby docks. Several males moved more tables and chairs to the edges of the room to expand the impromptu dance floor. The music got louder, and females wearing colorful scraps of clothes, some still in their work boots, filled the center of the space, while the males closed in and slowly positioned themselves in front of the person who drew their attention.

"Come dance." Bodi stood and wiggled her ample backside in a seductive swivel.

Veda shook her head and clung to her first drink.

Rhysa stood up and pointed at Blaize.

Blaize sipped her drink. "Not yet. You two go."

Bodi shrugged, grabbed Rhysa's hand, and pulled her through the tables to join the tight, gyrating crowd.

Veda tried to talk to Blaize, but the bar was loud and neither of them was very good at pointless conversation. Instead, they wordlessly agreed to watch their shipmates. Bodi was quickly surrounded by males trying to get her attention while she danced in her own personal world. A short while later, Rhysa came by the table for her drink and then rushed off to dive back into the group of males. Those two knew how to draw and keep male attention. But Blaize wasn't sure she wanted to learn the secret. It seemed like that just led to more opportunities to be left behind.

Once again, her glass was empty much sooner than it should have been. She looked at it carefully, held it up to the dim light. She didn't have a buzz, so she ordered another as soon as the server swung by their table.

"I need to use the facilities," she told Veda.

"I'll stay with the table." Veda wrapped her hands around her mostly full drink and shrank into her chair.

Blaize nodded, stood, and wobbled a bit. She quickly gripped the edge of the table when the room shimmied. Damn, the music must be loud to make the floor move. She had to focus to put her legs in the right order to move her across the room. She moved past the crowd toward the very back of the bar.

A Gordinian occupied a table nearby, and she recoiled. The noxious, hairy blob stood out in the crowd of dockworkers and ship crew. Gordinians were traders, merchants. The only thing they had to do with ships was greet them at the ports to get their stuff. She glanced at the others sitting with him and wrinkled her nose.

Who would do that voluntarily?

Varik.

She'd recognize his profile anywhere. Of course, he'd be meeting with a disgusting gasbag. Hell, he *was* one.

The other male made her pause, shifting deeper into the crowd for cover. Something about him was familiar, but she was sure she'd never met anyone from that weird swamp planet she couldn't recall the name of at that moment. No other beings had that particular gray-green sponginess. He turned slightly toward her, raising his arm to flag a server. Blaize narrowed her eyes as she inspected his face. Her gaze caught his, and his muddy gray eyes flashed white with black striations.

Her heart split in her chest, and she choked on a gasp.

Cifer.

Her lungs spasmed as she raced to the ladies' room.

The alcoholic contents of her stomach rushed up her throat. She'd suspected Cifer was bad news from the start. But she'd doubted herself. To be fair, he'd worked really hard to get her to trust him. And she had.

She groaned inside the stall she'd locked herself inside. So stupid. Part of her insisted she slink away and pretend she'd never met him. The other part, the drunk part, itched to punch him in the face for convincing her he might be a good guy. Was everything he'd told her a lie?

She'd take her proof to Dez. If Cifer was working with Varik, there was no way Cyra would want to transport him.

Maybe she could sneak out there and find an open table closer to the trio so she could hear what they were saying. Then she could get absolute evidence of Cifer's criminality—like stowing away hadn't been enough.

Rather than dwell on her mistake, she did her business and washed her hands, avoiding the mirror. If she didn't like what she saw, she couldn't do anything about it, so no point looking. She exited right into Cifer's arms.

"Blaize." His voice poured over her body like warm honey to pool in her panties.

She slapped his chest. "Let me go."

"Forgive me. I can explain. Not right now. But soon. I'll come to the ship."

"Don't bother. I'm telling Cyra. You won't be going with us."

"What are you talking about?"

"I'm talking about you being a criminal. Now I know." She hiccupped. "For sure. I knew before. But now I know."

"You're drunk."

"And I still know."

"You know that I want you. That you're the best thing that ever happened to me. That I adore you more than anything." He leaned in to kiss her.

She turned her head sharply. "You left me."

"It was important. I can explain." He stroked her hair. "Please. Just go back to your table. Don't let the males I'm with know that I know you."

"You mean Varik. The bastard." She pushed against his chest. "Cyra hates him almost as much as I do."

"Blaize. Please. I'll explain. But you have to stay safe. Take a sled. I'll pay."

"I don't want your dirty credits." She wrenched herself free and made it back to the table, where Veda was nearly asleep.

"Can we go?" Veda asked with a yawn.

"Hell yes." Blaize searched the dance floor for Rhysa or Bodi. Bodi was near the entrance with a male she had pressed against the wall. It looked like one of her hands was on his crotch. Blaize grabbed Veda's hand and pulled her through the crowd. She spoke to Bodi's back when they passed. "We're out."

Bodi held up her free hand in acknowledgement. Good enough. A short sled ride later, Blaize was back on the ship. She would talk to Cyra at first meal.

Cifer was as good as gone.

CHAPTER 20

Varik tracked Yonash as he rushed off to the restroom. What kind of amateur ass was this guy? You don't take a piss during a negotiation. A server hustled to the table, blocking Varik's view of the hall. Before he could tell the useless tool to fuck off, the foul-ass blob with the merchandise began asking about every brew the bar stocked. Varik scowled and considered walking away from the negotiations. Selling flesh was a loser's game, but there weren't many more profitable. Or riskier. A single sale was all well and good, but there were limitless opportunities there.

Corvus would be interested to know there was a new supplier trying to establish a foothold in the market. The pirate had made a fortune moving flesh and basically controlled the trade, limiting the supply to keep the prices high. He also kept a very low profile on Cassan, unlike the idiot sitting across from Varik. Sharing the name and location of the gaseous loser could be of value to Corvus. Maybe take away some of the debt he'd built up before he'd been able to leverage his relationships with Blaize and Auvi. Worth a favor, at least.

Varik had the credits to pay Corvus back in full, but it

would leave him low on funds. Maintaining the debt served him better. Varik leaned forward and grinned at the Gordinian.

The creature held up his hand. "No negotiations without both parties."

Varik clenched his jaw but swallowed his reaction.

Yonash dropped back into his chair. "Sorry about that. The beer here is so watered down, it went right through me." He grinned, and Varik wondered if the male was all that bright. "Let's talk price of goods." Yonash rubbed his hands together.

The man was a clown.

Varik threw out a number, a flat amount multiplied by the number of bodies he'd seen in the video.

Yonash pursed his lips and nodded at Varik.

What the fuck did that mean?

"Does the sale come with papers?" the clown asked.

"Of course." The Gordinian belched in what Varik assumed was a reaction to lying.

"Do the contracts expire when they age out? Are they transferable? I might want to auction the older one."

The Gordinian babbled about no limitations and excellent value.

"That's good," Yonash said. "Because the little ones aren't good for much, depending on where they hail from."

Varik was bored. He doubled the number.

Yonash scoffed. "I wouldn't give you more than—"

Yonash named a price so low, Varik's jaw dropped.

"Obviously, you have a better offer for this lot. But I suspect he's not a regular buyer, and he won't be back when he realizes you sold him inferior goods." Varik's competition shrugged.

Varik sputtered. *How dare he?*

"I'm headed to Chalcanth." Yonash dipped a nod in Varik's direction, as if to acknowledge what was obviously his birthplace. "They are quite prolific at producing hardy offspring, but it's not a wealthy planet. I think our arrangement might be better served if I became *your* supplier. Assuming you can get out of whatever deal brought you this shipment." The male leaned back in his chair and sipped his drink.

Everything was a game to this fool. He hadn't needed to piss. He hadn't even consumed his drink. And there were places on the station that would pay a premium for virgin flesh to be trained in a variety of service positions. Varik's vision went red and spotty. His gills flapped—something he never allowed to happen, especially in public. With a thrust of his hips, he scooted back his chair and barely restrained himself from flipping the table. "You have my final offer."

The Gordinian jumped up. "Yes, of course. I'll send a credit request. Where can I deliver the goods?"

Varik rattled off the berth where he'd docked *Cain's Alibi*. "I'll transfer half now in good faith. The rest when you deliver."

The bloated bug of a being wriggled in excitement, naming a time the following cycle.

Varik nodded in approval and left the table. A new plan formed as he stomped out of the bar. It would require some delicate timing and coordination. But he might have the pieces on the board to finally take Cyra down.

CHAPTER 21

Years of discipline allowed Cifer to calmly make his way to Master Corvus. His heart demanded he leave the negotiation table and follow Blaize. If it hadn't been for the children, he would have. But his brain ruled his body, and he had loaded the weapon that was Master. It would be far too dangerous to leave him cocked without verifying the direction he was pointed.

"Master." Cifer stood in front of the table.

"Sit." The old pirate's steely glare combined with the threat of his flanking bodyguards had Cifer pulling out the single empty chair and fitting himself onto the edge of it.

Silence filled the table for an uncomfortably extended period.

Corvus rolled his eyes. "Lose the disguise."

Cifer glanced around. The shadows would conceal his transformation from any casual observers. He slowly morphed into the coppery-skinned humanoid he most commonly adopted.

"I know what you really look like." The scowl on Corvus's face didn't have the effect on Cifer he might have hoped. Cifer had seen it too often.

The bodyguards shifted in their seats.

"The games you play are tedious. Besides, I taught you everything you know."

Cifer shrugged. They both knew the student had become the master, or Cifer would still be under Corvus's control.

"Fine. What did you learn?"

Cifer detailed what the Gordinian offered and the fact that Varik had committed to a premium price for the kids. "I'm not letting Varik take those kids off Cassan."

"Eh. Don't care. The kids are yours to do with as you wish. I'll be busy dealing with the Gordinian. How dare he transact business in my establishment without authorization."

Cifer held back a grin. The gas-bag slaver was well and truly fucked. He just didn't know it. Yet. So was Varik. Cifer hadn't missed the micro-reaction to the price Varik had agreed to pay. If he had to guess, Corvus was unhappy to discover that Varik had funds to spend while still owing a debt.

Cifer rose to leave.

"Don't be a stranger, son," Corvus spoke to Cifer's back.

Outside the bar, Cifer pulled out his data pad to check for an update from his spy.

Still no location of the ship Elaya had described. Cifer tapped back a message with the location and name of the ship that would receive the kids. *Keep an eye on it, but do not approach.*

He checked the time. It was too late to put the next part of his plan in motion. A couple of hours of sleep would serve him better than sitting in the dock outside a locked ship.

Blaize's head pounded all the way to the galley. She'd meant to get up earlier, but the alcohol swimming in her veins had made being vertical earlier impossible. The smell of Dez's cooking, usually so welcome, had bile rising in her throat. Puking was not going to make a difficult conversation easier. She swallowed tightly, forcing everything back down. Before she went into the galley, she took a couple of deep breaths in through her nose and out through her mouth. When she felt composed, she plastered a smile on her face and joined Captain Cyra and her mate.

"Blaize. How are you?" Cyra had the relaxed but energized appearance of a satisfied female. Blaize wasn't jealous at all. Nope, not a bit.

"I'm okay. Stayed out later than I should have."

"Oh, that explains why Veda isn't here." Cyra was speaking to Dez as if they were continuing a previous conversation.

The big bald male nodded without taking his eyes from the food preparation.

"Yeah. So. Um. There was something I saw at the bar that I wanted to talk to you about. It, um, concerns—"

"What did you see?" Dez placed a plate of food in front of her, and she swallowed hard and then forced herself to smile.

"I saw Varik."

Cyra and Dez both frowned.

"He was meeting with Cifer. And a Gordinian. I'm not sure who *he* was. But I know Cifer is up to no good, and I don't think we should take him on the ship anywhere. We don't know anything about him, and he's meeting with bad people. He's already stowed away, and we don't know what else he's done." Blaize took a deep breath and put some food on her fork that she would eat. Soon.

"Do you know what the meeting was about?" Dez asked.

"No."

"Did you ask Cifer about it?" Cyra asked.

"We didn't have time to talk. He said he'd explain, but what explanation could there be for meeting with Varik?"

"Varik left him on Kolben. Perhaps they were discussing the return of Cifer's credits." Dez spoke between bites of food, keeping one eye on Cyra, probably making sure she ate. Dez was a good male. Cyra was so lucky to have such an honorable male to care for her.

"We can't take him to Hiargus," Blaize blurted.

"You want to me cancel the contract?" Cyra looked at her sideways and wrinkled her brow. "That could ruin what little reputation we have. As it is, we haven't secured any other contract besides his. And that contract is very profitable."

"What does our reputation mean if we transport criminals? Are those the kinds of contracts we want? What if he's a killer and we're murdered in our sleep? What if he kills us just because he wants the ship? He could be anyone. And he's using children. One came to his rooms in the middle of the night, and he just ran off with her without a word."

Dez's eyes were wide when she was finally able to bite her tongue, literally, to stop the word vomit. When she'd felt green in the hallway, she'd had no idea that she was going to spew words instead of stale cocktails. Words she would do anything to erase from the mind of her captain and Dez.

"How do you know he left in the middle of the night with a child?" Dez's voice made Blaize's already shaky control evaporate. He was what she thought a father would sound like.

"I might have been at his place." Blaize pushed the fork around in her food.

"In the middle of the night?"

"Yes, sir." This was not the conversation she pictured having.

"Tell me about this child."

"Her name's Elaya. She used to be in the engineering academy at the orphanage that houses the pubescent females. I volunteer there." She looked up at Dez, hoping his expression had changed from stern parent. It hadn't. "Anyway, she—Elaya —left the program recently. She wasn't doing well, chafing under the rules according to the director, and really, they can't keep them against their will after a certain age. They have to want to be there. But there is such limited space, and the program has so much potential. I can't understand—"

"Blaize."

Babbling again. It was one of her worst habits.

"I recognized her voice before Cifer left. Without a word."

"You were intimate?" Dez asked.

Did she have to answer that? The heat flooding her system meant that she was turning red. She wouldn't even have to answer. He'd know.

"Yes." More breath than sound came out of her mouth. She stared at the floor.

"He just walked out without a word?" Cyra put her arm around Blaize.

Blaize nodded.

"Did he apologize or try to explain when he came back?"

Blaize looked up at Cyra's ocean eyes. "I got locked out. Varik came to his door, and when I opened it, he yanked me out. I got away from the asshole. I thought Cifer would come looking for me. Instead, I found him at the bar *with* Varik."

Dez sipped his caffeine before speaking. "I will speak with him. You don't have to be around him if you prefer. We can make modifications to the schedules."

"Is there no way you can cancel the contract? He's hanging out with Varik."

Cyra and Dez shared a wordless conversation. Then Cyra delivered their decision. "As much as it pains me to see you upset, I can't cancel a contract over a bad love affair. I wouldn't put it past Varik to create the illusion of an association to disrupt us."

"You weren't there." Blaize drew a breath to continue her argument, but Dez held out his hand and stopped her.

"Let me finish," Cyra said. "I know you believe he is doing criminal things, but we have no proof. Everything we've observed personally, beyond him stowing away, has been beneficial to the ship and the crew. I know a difficult personal relationship can color your opinion, but I have to do what's best for our business. He's already paid for transport to and from Hiargus in full. We have no valid reason to terminate the contract."

The conversation was over. Blaize could either quit or be trapped on the ship with Cifer for galactic months.

"Hiargus is a long journey. We're making at least two stops before we get there," Dez said.

Blaize looked at the captain.

Cyra scooped a forkful of her meal and made an obvious point of filling her mouth.

"What does that have to do with transporting him?"

He smiled. "It will give us time to assess his true purpose and provide two opportunities to turn him over to the authorities if he proves to be the criminal you believe he is."

The rest of the meal passed in silence and settled in Blaize's stomach like a greasy brick.

Dez paused at the door. "By the way, we've had Bodi investigating Cifer's past. She's found nothing."

"So he's a smart criminal," Blaize said under her breath, but Dez and Cyra had already left.

She tidied the remnants of her meal and stomped back to her quarters. She could use a long shower before she started on the preflight checklist. It was a full cycle's worth of work, if she didn't sleep or eat. The tasks would keep her mind off a certain shifting criminal who had slithered past her defenses. In fact, she could do a workshop on ship preparation for the academy. That would take her mind off his presence.

She could avoid him completely for the entire trip. He was going to be sleeping in the crew quarters, so it wasn't like she'd have to walk by his cell every morning. She barely saw the rest of the crew, other than at meals, except for Veda in her greenhouse. Dez's meals would be missed, but she'd been putting on weight with his excellent cuisine. A couple of months of protein bars and water would do her good.

She let the warm spray wash over her. A plan. Everything looked better when she had a plan.

CHAPTER 22

"Normally, on a standard ship, you would have different engineers to do the various jobs, like the PHALCON or Booster Engineer. But it's important that you are proficient in as many positions as possible because this increases your value to the crew and captain, and you're qualified to apply for more jobs." Blaize met the eye of each of the five girls she'd picked up earlier in the day for some hands-on training. She loved working with the budding engineers, knowing that because of their hard work and the opportunities she was helping to provide, their futures would be so much brighter. They'd lost a few of the students, Elaya for example, but the eagerness of these five more than made up for it.

One of the girls raised her hand.

"Yes?" Blaize wasn't used to hand raising to get her attention.

"What's a falcon?"

"That's an abbreviation for power, heating, articulation, and lighting controls. It's the crew member who basically oversees the environmental systems. It's more about the internal systems to keep the crew alive, versus navigational or power systems used for flight."

The girl nodded and made notes on her handheld.

"How many engineers does this ship have?" The girl with bright purple hair didn't wait to raise her hand.

"One. Me."

"Seriously?" She swiveled her head, looking around the main engine rooms where they stood. "This ship is huge. I mean, how?"

"I do a lot of things proactively, and I have a lot of checklists." Blaize shrugged. And she was used to working alone and worked twice as hard to even be accepted as an engineer. These females didn't know how blessed they were to be in an all-girl academy.

She divided up the team, giving them checklists to complete. She rotated the teams so that she could work with each one individually over the course of the time they had. Too soon, it was over and time to take them back to the academy for last meal. They chattered in the sled all the way back. Blaize was both sad and relieved to see them go. It was inspiring to work with them, to see the next generation develop, but it was exhausting to answer all their questions and make sure no errors were made. Although they were seniors and had done a great job, in the end, it was her ass that was going to be on the ship. There were no do-overs in space.

She dragged herself from the sled and up the gangplank. No matter how tired she was, she needed to do a little more, had to go back down to her precious systems. It wasn't about going by Cifer's old cell. But she couldn't help but step in and look around. It felt like part of him was still there, which didn't make a ton of sense. Dez had used this cell too before Cyra had accepted him. But Blaize had no sense of Dez's presence, only Cifer's. She dropped onto the bunk for a quick rest, just for a moment. His scent was still on the pillow, just like it had been in his apartment. Drawing a deep breath in through her nose, she let his essence flow through her before she closed her eyes and slept.

Cifer shook her gently. "Wake up, Beauty."

Blaize rolled over and rubbed her eyes. "Where were you?"

"Had some business to take care of." He laid his body over hers and kissed her, his tongue tangling with hers. His spicy taste satisfied a craving she didn't know she had. They moaned in unison. He drew down the zipper on her suit. For some reason, she wasn't wearing a bra, and her breasts sprang free, nipples hard, demanding his attention. He didn't leave her wanting. He rolled one nipple between his thumb and first two fingers as he descended on the other with his hot, wet mouth. Blaize arched her back into his touch. It wasn't enough. She ran her fingers through his coarse dark locks and pulled him tighter to his body. His touch was perfect, intense without being painful. He released her wet nipple into the cold air and moved to the other sensitized bud. He was going to make her come just from playing with her chest. She pressed her thighs together, trying to relieve the achy want at her core.

Cifer released the nipple he'd been teasing with his fingers and pressed his hand firmly between her legs. It was like he'd read her mind, or at least her body.

"Yes," she moaned, parting her legs.

Cifer's palm was on her mound, and his fingers pulsed and pinched her lips through her suit. Why wouldn't he take off her clothes? They needed to be naked. He needed to be inside her again. She needed to come around his cock again and again. He pressed harder and nipped her breast. The orgasm wasn't an explosion... It was a series of small detonations that snuck up on her and resonated deep inside before a rush of hot cream filled her panties and darkness filled her vision.

She opened her squinted eyes, staring at the ceiling of the cell, completely alone. But her panties were wet, and she was panting for air. Her nipples were as hard as stone but covered by her crew uniform.

A dream.

It had been a stupid sex dream.

She had to get out of this cell. It was just another space in the bowels of the ship, nothing special. It was ridiculous to be drawn to a space that didn't contain the object of her desire. And as far as the desire went, that was the stupidest thing of all. She had to survive the trip to Hiargus.

She should return to her quarters to take another shower and get some rest. Yet, there was still a ton of work to do before they would be ready to take off. Working with the students had been rewarding but inefficient. There would be no more time to fantasize if they wanted to take off on time. Cyra probably wouldn't care, but it would embarrass Blaize to miss a deadline. So, a few hours of sleep, and then she would get back to the most important thing in her life, *The Treasure*. Maybe Cifer would find something to keep him on station, and they wouldn't even have to go to Hiargus.

Blaize slunk back to her quarters, making sure to check around corners before taking any turn. It wouldn't do to run into Cifer with soaked panties from a wet dream about him. Not that he would know the dream was about him, but she would.

Fortune was with her, and she made it to the peaceful isolation of her bare cabin. She did a quick wash, where she had to resist the temptation to finger herself to the image of Cifer between her legs. She was hopeless. In bed, she recited the power equations she'd learned in school, hoping sleep would finally take her away.

Just as she was about to drift off, she heard voices in the corridor. He was there. Her heart raced. Cifer was on the ship, and he was reclaiming the room next to hers.

———

Blaize did her best to tiptoe through the corridors on her way to the galley. The dread at the thought of seeing him was quickly replaced by disappointment when she reached the empty room. Blaize chastised herself for caring and opened the cabinet that contained the protein bars. She grabbed three, prepared to spend the entire cycle rerunning the checklists.

"Hi, Blaize."

The soft voice startled her, and she fumbled with the bars. "Veda. Where is everyone? I expected to be late for the meal again, but it seems like I'm either way too late or possibly early. That never happens."

Veda smiled. "You didn't miss anything. Dez didn't cook because Rhysa stayed with Gareth to keep *negotiating* our fuel rate. And Bodi had errands to run before we leave. Dez and Cyra have been locked away in their quarters since very early, when Cifer left."

"Cifer was here?" She'd known that, but maybe playing ignorant would yield some info.

"He met with the captain and Dez last night. I'm not sure of the details, but it seems like there was some problem he needed to take care of before he can travel."

Blaize bit back a variety of uncharitable answers. They would only make Veda uncomfortable. "Right. Well, I'll be in the engine room if anyone needs me." Blaize took a few steps to the door and paused. "Also, I'm sending a load to the laundry service—coveralls, sheets, and towels—if you have anything."

"Oh, yes. It takes so long to process the big stuff with our onboard machines."

"Leave the pile by the bay door. I'll make the arrangements. If you see anyone else, let them know."

"Thank you, Blaize."

Veda's warm approval stayed with Blaize for several hours, until she realized that she'd completed reviewing the checklists. The girls had done an admirable job. She'd stripped the cell bedding and her own and arranged for the service pickup, and still Cifer was gone. She shouldn't notice that. Rather than stare at the cold, empty cell for a moment longer, she went to find the captain. To tell her about the laundry run. Nothing else. Not a word about Cifer.

But as she turned the corner, Dez rushed forward, and Blaize had to sidestep quickly to avoid being run over.

"What's wrong?"

Dez kept moving without a word.

Cyra emerged from her quarters. "Cifer is in trouble."

"What?"

Cyra moved past Blaize toward the bridge. Dez raced for the exit.

Bodi was at the communication station. Cyra curled around behind her to stare at the screen. "Do you see Dez?"

Bodi pointed at the screen where a dot moved along a map of the station. "Here."

"Good. Don't lose him."

Blaize stomped her foot and bellowed, "What is going on?"

Cyra stood and blinked at Blaize. Her gills flapped. "Cifer made us promise that if he wasn't back by a specific time, we should contact the authorities. But we did that, and they don't seem to care. So Dez is going after him."

"How are you going to find him among the millions of beings on the station? He could be anywhere." Blaize tried to breathe, but her heart was beating so hard, her lungs couldn't make room for air in her chest.

Cyra held out a data pad. "We put a tracker on his pad, but it stopped moving, and then it went dead. Dez is going to the last place it pinged."

"Dez went by himself?"

Without waiting for an answer, Blaize ran for the toolbox in her engine room. She grabbed the huge wrench she'd used for securing the shelves and lights with Veda and ran out of the ship. On the way, she called Bodi on her comm.

"What?"

"Send me Dez's tracker info. He can't go by himself. He has one hand."

Dez had barely survived Varik's last attack. If Blaize had to break rules and crack skulls to protect her captain's mate, then she would.

It had nothing to do with Cifer being at risk. At all.

CHAPTER 23

Varik settled into his captain's chair. It was the most comfortable spot on his ship, which he didn't dare leave, even to rest in his rented room. Everything was going to plan. The cargo had been loaded. The next step: figure out how to get the crates of whiny kids on Cyra's ship. Shouldn't be that difficult. She seemed to have no trouble getting contracts. When he'd last spied on her, there had been a crew offloading pallets from the Kolben Mining Company. The fact that she was getting jobs so easily only served to motivate him even more. That bitch would pay for stealing his ship and for whatever she'd done to Jarn.

"Captain," Karnek interrupted. "Something's got the little fuckers agitated. They're squirming around and acting weird."

Varik crossed to the display at Karnek's station. "What's going on?"

The door to one of the crates opened. Varik ran toward the small cargo hold, Karnek close behind.

One of the brats ran and dropped from the open cargo door, not waiting for the ramp to lower. How the fuck had that opened? The rest were screaming.

"Check the locks." Varik lurched toward the nearest crate.

Karnek fell back with an audible rush of air. Varik caught movement from the corner of his eye. He pivoted and swung his fist in an arc, connecting with flesh. A male materialized out of thin air. The same male that had exited *The Treasure* instead of Jarn. Cifer. That was the name Corvus had given him. Too bad he hadn't mentioned the fucker could go invisible. A fist knocked all other thoughts from Varik's head as he reeled back, balance lost.

Cifer's limbs shot out, and his eyes widened before he dropped into a pile of flesh and bone, barely blinking.

"Got him." Karnek grinned, holding up an electric stunner.

Varik reflected his grin and kicked Cifer in the gut. "Put him in the crate."

Karnek lifted Cifer's piss-covered legs, and Varik latched on to the invader's shoulders, dragging his still-twitching body into the empty crate. Not a horrible trade, but he'd have to rethink moving the crates to *The Treasure*. A passel of whiny brats that didn't speak Galaxian was one thing. A fully grown male who could identify Varik presented an entirely different challenge.

"Find the next flesh auction. Make sure Kolben Mining will be there. But not just their auction. I'll have to offload the brats too."

Karnek answered as he left the cargo. "Aye, Captain."

"Wait." The faint sound barely reached Varik's ears. He turned his head toward Cifer.

"You don't want to do this." His eyes were wide, breath coming in pants. "I'm worth more than a single auction price. I have skills."

For a grown man who recovered quickly from electrocution, he seemed panicked to be in a cage. He'd create more of a fuss than the brats if left as he was. Varik went to a cabinet and retrieved the sedative that hadn't been necessary for the kids.

He doubled the dose and held the injection wand down by the side of his leg. Careful to stay out of arms reach, he neared the overstuffed crate. "What skills are those?"

Cifer drew a large breath. His chest heaved, and his eyes closed. Varik had something that would calm him faster than any breathing technique. He jabbed the wand between the bars and nailed Cifer in the upper arm. Perfect hit. The rapid injector finished delivering the dosage before Varik could retract the device. A split second passed. Cifer's eyes went wide, changing color to white with black lines, and then his lids shuttered and his body slumped.

Varik whistled a tune as he stored the injection wand. One of his smarter purchases, even if he had used it in an unplanned way. He left the softly crying kids huddling in the corners of their crates. Sometimes an example was more effective than punishment. He'd have no more problems with his cargo.

CHAPTER 24

BASED on the speed at which Blaize was losing Dez, he had to be in a sled. She flagged down a transport.

"Where to?" the robotic voice asked.

Blaize checked the tracker. The only logical place Dez could be headed, based on the map with his glowing dot, was the remote garbage docks. The ones used mainly for offloading nonrecyclable waste to distant, uninhabitable planets. She voiced the command. Of course, Varik would be hanging out in what amounted to a dumpster.

She dug her fingers into her thigh to stop herself from rattling her foot against the vehicle platform. There was no way to make it go faster. The wrench rested on her lap. She clutched her data pad in the other hand, each moment making her more certain of Dez's destination. Would have been helpful if Cyra had told her where Dez was going. But it wasn't like she'd given the captain a chance.

Finally, the sled stopped at the entrance to the dumpster docks—the same place Dez had paused. He'd moved much slower since that moment. Blaize authorized the credit transfer and raced to catch up. As Cifer had explained, she wasn't able to hide, so she might as well barge in. She caught up to Dez talking to a crying child, huddled behind a foul-smelling clunky ship that had probably been transporting the worst kind of waste for galactic years. Blaize swallowed back her gorge.

"Dez?"

He startled and glanced up with narrowed yellow eyes. His gray skin blended better than her own.

"Get down."

Blaize crouched, using the length of the wrench as a prop. Dez gave her a puzzled look before returning his attention to the child.

"Do you remember what the ship looked like?" Dez asked in a gentle tone.

The kid shook his head.

"Big or small?" Blaize asked.

The child glanced around. "Small."

Blaize gave him an approving smile. "Dirty or clean?"

"Clean?"

"Very good. That's so helpful."

The child gave a shaky nod.

"Okay, last question." Because a kid that age with that much trauma could only be expected to do so much. "Can you point to where you think it might be?"

With a nod, the child spun, hesitated, and then thrust out a finger.

"That's so good. I'm going to get a sled to take you to a friend of mine. Have you ever ridden in a sled?"

The child nodded, surprising Blaize. "Will you be okay to find my friend? I'm going to text her to tell her to expect you. She'll be waiting when the sled stops."

Another shaky nod. Blaize fired off a text to Director Glinchart with a line of explanation and a promise to tell all later. She pinned Dez with a glare. "Wait for me."

Dez opened his mouth, closed it, and nodded.

Thankfully, the sled she'd arrived in hadn't been contracted. She uploaded the address and her credits. "You're going to be okay."

The child's wide-eyed gaze ripped through her chest. The urge to get in the vehicle and see him safely to the orphanage was difficult to fight. But there were likely more kids. And Blaize had to find out how Cifer was involved. Because if he had anything to do with making that child cry, she was going to brain him with the wrench and have zero regrets. Well, maybe one. Sleeping with him. But she'd carried the regret of Varik for galactic years. Cifer wouldn't be that much more emotional weight.

As soon as the sled was moving, Blaize raced back to Dez.

"I think Cifer is on one of the ships."

"His tracker isn't here, is it?" Blaize had more to say, but that was the most important question.

"I found his abandoned pad at the entrance. Not sure why he would have left it."

Blaize could guess. He was up to shady shit, and he didn't really want Dez and Cyra to know. Same as when he'd left her at his apartment.

Crouched over, Dez slow-walked along the dumpster ships.

Blaize mimicked his movements, but there was no hiding her hair, as Cifer had helpfully pointed out. A flash of the moment in the mirror when he'd taken on her coloring and she'd blended perfectly took over her vision. She blinked it away.

Dez froze and lowered himself farther. Blaize did the same. He held a finger to his lips. Like she was going to talk at a moment like that. Although she did have plenty of questions. Dez pointed, and Blaize traced the imaginary vector to a shiny ship with hardly a scratch on it, as if it hadn't spent much time in space. She shifted past Dez to get a different angle. *Cain's*

Alibi. That's the ship that had attacked them—Varik's vessel. That weasel.

She gripped her wrench tighter.

Dez moved around behind her. The ship was closed up tight. Whatever method the kid had used to escape, it was likely Varik was aware of the loss and had battened down the hatches. Dez wrapped his hand around his stump and stared at the ship as if he could read it somehow.

Blaize stood up, marched over to the ship, and raised her wrench. She brought it down with her full strength just below the area where the bridge jutted out from the main hull. Again. And again. She lifted the wrench to continue when a strong hand stopped her.

"What are you doing?" Dez hissed from where he still crouched.

"Knocking." Blaize tilted her head. The crew ramp lowered, and Varik emerged, looking nearly purple with rage.

Blaize grinned at Dez. "Guess they're home."

Dez whipped out his data pad, rested it on his thigh, and tapped out a message.

Blaize marched toward Varik, wrench held like a club. "Where's Cifer?"

"You fucking crazy bitch. You're going to pay for that."

"Doubt it. You'd have to call the authorities. And knowing you, that isn't an option because you have to be the vilest criminal asshole I know. All I'm curious about is if Cifer is working for you or against you." Before she could continue, a male came racing past Varik, a stunner in hand. As he lunged for Blaize, she swung as hard as she could. Teeth fountained out of his mouth, and he dropped into a heap. Her distraction allowed Varik to sneak up on her, but a single gray arm wrapped around his neck and tugged him off his feet.

Blaize continued up the ramp. Over her shoulder, she told Varik, "Purple is a good color for you."

Inside the ship, there were two options. One upward-sloping hall led to the bridge. She pivoted to the aft door. A single unsecured button made the thin panel slide back. A cramped space filled with metal cages enraged her more than she already had been.

She would kill Varik. The wrench weighed heavy in her hands as she moved to the first cage. The oldest child stared up at her from his knees. He couldn't even stand up in the too-small space.

"Move back and cover your face."

The child didn't move.

"I'm going to get you out." She flapped her hand to shoo him back and mimed covering her own head.

Finally, the boy moved back. Blaize whacked the biometric lock on the cage. It took two hits before it shattered, and she was able to sweep the door open. Without waiting, she moved to the next cage. The little one was already in position. At the third cage, she froze. Instead of a child, she found Cifer, smelling foul and completely unconscious. She bashed the lock, her heart racing, hoping he didn't catch any shrapnel. Although the door opened, he still didn't move, except for a slight rise and fall of his chest. Alive.

A wave of relief washed over her. She may have felt like killing him at a point or two in the last cycle, but that didn't mean she really wanted him dead.

Without Dez, she wouldn't be able to move him, and there were still two more kids to free. Once they were all out, she guided them back through the doorway. Dez had turned over Varik to the uniformed port guards. Medics were lifting the toothy asshole into an emergency service sled.

"Wait," she called out to them. "There's one more. He's

unconscious. I don't know from what, but he needs help, and I can't get him out of the cage by myself." Just because Cifer was in a cage didn't exonerate him. Varik turned on his partners all the time. She should know. But she couldn't leave Cifer there like that. One of the medics clambered into the sled next to the toothless guy, and the other met Blaize at the end of the ramp.

"Show me."

"He's breathing, and I don't see any obvious issues. I mean, besides the fact that he's not talking or opening his eyes or moving. But I mean, he's not bleeding, and nothing is at an odd angle. I don't have any medical training, though. I'm an engineer." She held up the wrench. "Tools and tech, not blood and guts." And then she clamped her mouth shut, her cheeks heating.

The medic stayed silent but followed her.

Cifer stood out because—holy fuck.

She hadn't noticed it before, but his skin wasn't copper... It was green and kind of scaly. And he wasn't as bulky as he had been, and— She blinked. Something besides a foot had emerged from one of his pant legs. What *was* he?

The medic had crouched beside him, blocking some of her view, but there was no mistaking that he had a tail. So besides being able to change his coloring, he could change his shape. Green and scaly with a tail was his natural shape? Spots dotted her vision, and she lowered herself to the floor and put her head between her knees. She'd had sex with him. He hadn't had a tail then. Had he?

She flashed to the moment he'd teased her ass. *Had he?*

Her distress wasn't about how he looked. He was still a perfectly cut, sexy example of masculinity, but she'd been intimate with a lie.

"Where am I?"

She lifted her head. The medic had moved back, and Cifer

was crawling out of the cage, looking exactly as he had the entire time she'd known him. No tail. Scaleless copper skin. Bulky muscles.

A quick glance at the medic did nothing to confirm or refute that she'd lost her mind.

Dez appeared at her side from nowhere. "Are you okay?"

He held out his hand, and she let him guide her to standing.

"You saved me," Cifer told him.

"I believe Blaize has to take most of the credit."

Cifer reached for her, gliding his fingers along her face to shift her hair back. She stepped out of his reach. "Beauty," he sighed. "Thank you."

"I came for the kids. You just happened to be here. And after I get the kids to the orphanage and under the director's care, I'd like to know how exactly you ended up here with Varik, with kids in cages, and why you have a freaking tail." She recognized that her voice had taken on an unhinged tone, but she couldn't help it. Rather than try to get control, she stomped off to deal with the one thing she could handle.

The kids.

CHAPTER 25

IT HAD BEEN over a galactic week since Cifer had been alone with Blaize. She'd been successfully avoiding him. He lingered in an alcove in the corridor, letting himself blend into the wall, hoping to catch sight of the female who had burned herself into his heart. Aside from a few meals shared with the entire crew where she had barely said two words to him, nothing. She'd ghosted him. It was a tribute to her ingenuity that she could hide so well when they were limited to the expanse of one spaceship. Granted, the ship was large, but it wasn't a space station.

For most of his life, he'd been reacting to the fact that he'd been abducted from his home planet by pirates. And to stay alive, he'd done horrible things. His past made him a bad guy, but he didn't feel like a horrible person. The crimes he'd committed were about survival. As soon as he could, he liberated himself from Master Corvus. Too bad it wasn't before he'd witnessed Master kill someone. No matter how much time had passed or the fact it hadn't been by his hand, that life would always weigh on his conscience. That life was the reason he'd worked so hard to free himself from Master's mercies.

He spent most of his credits taking care of other kids like

him so they didn't get caught in a situation like he had. Even the jobs he took were focused on righting wrongs. Like breaking into the Kolben Mining Corporate offices to steal the orb. Or pretending to be a flesh peddler to get kids out of the market.

They would be landing soon on the planet Din' Gale. Dez's home. Maybe he could find a moment to be alone with Blaize. Cifer had so much he needed to say. An apology for leaving after their supernova night together was only the start of the list. And he owed her a thank-you for saving his life, because if she hadn't saved him from Varik's cage, he could have already been sold.

A flash of red caught his attention. Was Blaize tiptoeing through the corridor? He laughed loudly, unable to hold back, and stepped into her path. "Avoiding me, Beauty?"

She jumped a foot into the air and squealed. "You scared me."

"And you never walk softly. What's up?"

"Nothing." She put her head down and tried to stomp around him, but he moved to block her.

"I want to talk to you."

"There's nothing you have to say that I need to hear."

"I disagree." Cifer shuddered out a breath, searching for the right words. This conversation was critical. "Let me explain. Apologize."

"I have a ship to run. You're a guest. Why don't you go find some entertainment and relax?" She dodged around him and ran down the hall.

"This isn't done," he called after her. The fact that she was afraid enough to run meant her feelings were just as strong as his. If she felt nothing, she wouldn't have to avoid him. He smiled for the first time since their night together. He could outwait her.

They were meant to be together. Apart, they were both unhappy. And the longing kept him up at night. If he believed begging had any chance of working at all, he'd be on his knees outside her door. That wouldn't work. He was determined to figure out what would.

He headed in the opposite direction from where she'd gone. A workout might release some of his frustration. He paused on the way, picking up a washer peeking out from the seam of the passageway and tucking it into his pocket.

Cifer pressed his face to the portal as they broke through the cloud cover, and he had his first in-person look at the planet Dez had called home, Din' Gale. It called to the place in his soul that remembered anything about his home planet. It was lush and green. There was a clearing for their pod to land and a stunning octagonal building with the spaceport controls and crew. The wood and glass structure seemed to grow from the landscape.

"It's beautiful, is it not?" Dez's voice broke through Cifer's trip to the past. They were the only two not on the bridge.

"How did you ever leave?"

"Love," Dez replied, like it was the most obvious answer.

It was. Probably the only answer, aside from being stolen away, that could've made any sense. Cifer didn't know Dez's story, but his love for the captain was obvious.

"Wait until you see the land around my family's home. This will pale in comparison."

Cifer nodded, unable to form words that wouldn't betray his emotions.

As soon as the ship landed, Cifer followed Dez to the ramp

out of the ship. The same ramp Cifer had used to sneak onto *The Treasure* on a completely different planet.

He glanced over his shoulder for Blaize. He wanted to share the experience of Din' Gale with her, to see what she thought. It was her second trip to the planet, but surely she remained impressed. Her eyes were on his, and the corners of her mouth quirked up before she quickly looked away.

Cifer walked with the crew across the tarmac and into the window-laden building.

"Dez!" A small woman with lighter coloring than Dez and deep-red markings darted across the open floor plan in the spaceport, her long black hair flowing behind her as she launched herself. Dez caught her one-handed easily, his stump stuffed in his pants pocket. Cyra, holding Princess on a lead, was smiling widely, giving them plenty of room.

"My sister, how are you?" He kissed her cheek before setting her back on the floor. Another man, not quite as big as Dez, but bald and with similar dark markings, stepped forward, wrapping his arm around Dez's sister and putting his hand out in greeting to Dez. Cifer wasn't sure who this probable brother-in-law was, but based on the jewels and fine fabrics, Dez's sister had married well.

"Your Highness, greetings," Dez said formally as they grasped each other. Dez then introduced Cifer to the prince and his sister, as well as his mother, Azhume, and father, Daymuhnd.

Cifer wasn't sure how to act around a family. He observed the others and tried to blend in. Cyra was obviously well loved by the family, although according to what Veda had told him, this was only her second visit, and the first one had been to transport Dez to Kolben.

Daymuhnd's face settled into a grim mask. "Show us."

Dez stiffened at his father's command. Azhume gripped her husband's arm and stared at her son.

"It's not a big deal." Dez stepped back.

"Brother. You lost your hand," his sister exclaimed.

"An appendage. Not my life."

"But I'm the cause." Tears filled his sister's eyes.

Cyra shifted closer to Dez.

"That is not true. A man with a bomb was the cause. I'm honored to have protected my mate and her crew. This could have just as easily happened here in a farming accident." Dez removed his arm from his pocket. "I'm perfectly fine. Able to function in all ways."

"Dez and I are looking into options. Fine-motor robotics are incredibly sophisticated. With the right doctors..." Cyra trailed off.

Dez squeezed her in a one-armed embrace.

"You will allow me to help with the cost." The prince's tone was a royal edict.

"Your kind offer is most welcome," Cyra replied before Dez could open his mouth.

Azhume stepped into the gap between the residents and the visitors. She held out her arm and addressed Cifer. "Come. You must dine with us. We are celebrating."

"What are we celebrating this time?" Dez asked with a hint of laughter in his voice.

"Your freedom, your mating, your survival, your new friend." She gave a warm smile to Cifer.

He hoped Dez's father didn't take offense. He might be older than Cifer, but he was huge. Cifer checked over Azhume's head. Her male laughed, clearly at ease with his family's antics. Cifer followed the tiny gray woman.

The meal was unlike anything Cifer had experienced in his life. Not even dim memories from his childhood could compete. The dishes were fresh, the flavors unfamiliar and yet so incredible. He'd had to make an effort to participate in the conversation instead of focusing solely on the food. At the point he couldn't eat another bite, he glanced around the table, unsure who his host was—Dez's parents or the Prince and Princess. Didn't matter. "Thank you for this delicious meal. Incredible flavors and such bounty." It occurred to him he was dining with royalty. "Does everyone eat like this?"

The prince wiped his hands and placed his napkin next to his own empty plate. "The farmlands on the far side of the planet are quite fertile, and the terrain is more conducive to farming than these rocky lands."

Cifer had been impressed with the rocky peaks and waterfalls as they'd traveled from the spaceport to the royal homes. But as beautiful as the land was, it wasn't farmable. At least not easily. Veda could probably figure out a way to do it.

The prince had leaned over his wife to speak to Dez. "In fact, the crops have been so successful this year, I would like to discuss another shipment."

"Of course. Cifer, will you join us?" Dez asked.

Shocked, he stood when the prince and Dez did, and they excused themselves from the remainder of the group. The males led him back to a lavish office, lined with books and comfortable chairs in addition to the mandatory work desk.

The prince poured three glasses of a blue-green liquid that looked as potent as it smelled. Cifer didn't often drink, but he recognized the requirement in this situation. It seemed there was going to be a business discussion, and Dez had told him earlier that he wanted Cifer to help out in these dealings as part of his payment for travel to Hiargus. It was an easy trade.

"Dez, I'm unsure how to proceed. Your sister and I owe you so much. A debt that could never be repaid."

"There is no debt, Your Highness."

"It's ridiculous for my brother to call me Your Highness. Please. Call me Cauhdin."

Dez nodded with a slight tilt to show his neck.

"Where do you travel next?" The prince sipped his drink, a small sip.

Cifer did the same and nearly spit it across the room. It was sweet, but the flame that danced across his tongue made his nose tingle and his eyes water. Even the insides of his ears itched.

"It's an acquired taste," Dez said. He sipped from his own glass and closed his eyes as if he were enjoying the burning fuel. After a long moment, he replied to Cauhdin. "We're traveling to Chalcanth. It is time for Cyra to visit her own family, and then we will embark for Hiargus."

"Hiargus?" the prince snapped and sat up, leaning forward. "What demon possession would compel you to go all the way there?"

"It's my fault, Your Highness. I have some business there." Cifer didn't want Dez to do all the talking for him.

"What kind of business are you in?"

"I am a retriever. I find things or, occasionally, beings, and bring them back." It was the easiest explanation.

"Hmm. Interesting business. I can see the possibilities. But Hiargus?"

"It was a lucrative contract with a generous timeline." Cifer lifted one shoulder in a shrug.

"Chalcanth has possibilities for produce delivery." Dez changed the topic back to the original purpose, and Cifer could have kissed the male in relief. He didn't like talking about his work, especially to royals and other official-type beings.

They continued their discussion. Cifer was given the task of determining a fair price for their goods and of reaching out to wholesalers who could offload the merchandise quickly. Dez didn't seem to want to be involved at all.

"I'll make those calls as soon as possible." Cifer had an old contact on the water planet, but it had been a while since they'd spoken.

"Don't rush. We have time. Enjoy the rest of your time here."

Cifer wasn't going to waste a minute of enjoying Din' Gale. If the calls could wait, he could go exploring and ruminate on how to convince Blaize to give him another chance. "I think I'll get some air, then."

"There is a path leading from the back lower level. If you follow it toward the woods, it will take you to one of my favorite places. I would guide you, but I must find my mate." Dez wobbled the tiniest bit when he stood.

Cifer continued down the stairs while Dez went in search of Cyra.

The air outside was moist and rich with the sounds of insects and birds. It was beautiful. It could only have been better if Blaize were with him. Maybe before they left for Chalcanth, they could spend some time together outdoors. She had told him she didn't go out in the sun much, and he could understand that, given her fair skin, but this path was heavily shaded.

Lost in his thoughts and the landscape, he wasn't sure how long he'd been walking when he froze, his breath leaving him in a gust of longing. Blaize, posed in front of the most beautiful waterfall he'd ever seen. It would have been stunning without her—the height, the rocks framing the water, jutting into it to cause pronounced cascades on top of the base. The sunlight caught the sprays and made them sparkle and come alive with color. But there was no color more breathtaking than his female, her hair looking like flames in the sunlight. A noise, possibly the pounding of his heart, made her look back over her shoulder.

"Blaize." The word escaped with the intensity of all the time he'd spent aching for her, all the explanations and apologies she hadn't accepted.

"What are you doing here?" She whipped around and clutched her sides protectively.

"I didn't know you'd be here, but I'm glad you are." He approached her slowly, as if she were a dangerous, injured beast who might strike at any moment. "I have so much I want to say. I miss you so much. Miss talking with you. Working with you. Kissing you." He tilted his head toward her, a breath of space between their lips.

CHAPTER 26

Blaize pressed her lips to Cifer's. He startled before deepening the connection. She poured all her longing and doubts back into him as their tongues tangled. He was warm and spicy, temptation and alarm. She'd spent years alone without the ache that had wriggled its way into the spaces of her heart. He caressed her cheek, running his fingers through her hair. The urge to succumb to his possessive touch, to cast aside all the warnings and dive into him, rolled over her.

But nothing had changed. He was still who he was. She blamed the romantic location, the way his skin shimmered in the forest light, the way her heart pounded around him, dampening all logic. But she wasn't impulsive. She didn't kiss bad boys. She didn't let her heart lead. Not again.

She broke away, shoving him, and stepped back.

He staggered, the look on his face as if he'd been stabbed. "What?"

"I can't, Cifer." She struggled for a calm breath and searched for an explanation. "I can't be with someone like you."

"What are you talking about, someone like me?"

The pain in his tone made her second-guess her decision for a split second. But she couldn't break the rules, especially the ones she'd set for herself. The ones she'd made so she'd never be hurt again. "You're a thief, a criminal. Or you associate with criminals, and you break the law, which technically makes you a criminal. And you left me, went off with a girl. *You left me*. Without a word. And then I find you in the bar with Varik, and the next thing I know, you're mixed up in kidnapping children. And then there's the fact that I don't even know what you truly look like. I've seen you naked, and I don't know. How is that possible? And don't tell me I imagined your tail. The altered skin coloring wasn't surprising, but a tail? Seems like something a lover should know about. Especially—"

"I'm sorry, Beauty." Cifer stepped toward her, but she held out her hand to stop him. "I should have explained. I planned to be back before you realized I was gone. To wake you when I returned. To love you again." Sadness and regret filled his gaze.

She'd been fooled by soft looks before. "What about the bar? You and Varik?"

Cifer stepped closer.

She didn't move, and he wrapped her in his arms. The weight of his presence anchored her in place when she should be running.

"I'm sorry I left. So sorry. Words can't begin to describe the depth of my regret when I returned and you were gone."

She shivered.

"You're cold."

Although the sun was sinking in the sky, the shadows were much longer, and the spray coming off the waterfall had dampened her clothes, her reaction wasn't to the temperature. Her tremors were caused by the war between wanting him and the certainty that it would be her downfall. She let him lead her back to the house where they were staying. When they neared his room, she pulled out of his arms. "I have to go."

"Wait. Give me a chance—"

She shook her head. "I need to change and then run through some system checks. We're taking off soon, and I need to check on the ship."

"But I still need to explain everything."

Not a chance they'd do any talking if she let him lead her through his door. A second time would only give her twice as much to regret. "I have responsibilities."

"Would you like my help?" His soft question hung in the hall between them.

She corralled all the weakness for him and shoved it down deep. "There's nothing you can do."

He leaned in to kiss her, but she turned at the last second and his lips ended up on her cheek, leaving a warm mark she wanted to press her fingers to, holding it against her skin. She curled her hands into fists, spun, and strode away without looking back, despite how desperately her body ached for one more glance.

Giving in at the waterfall had been a mistake. No matter how much she burned for him, she'd given herself boundaries, and she'd broken them. Crossed line after line. And not just the kiss. She'd broken into Varik's ship, smashed the locks. She could have been arrested. An arrest record would kill her chances of being employed on most ships if Cyra ever ended their partnership.

Who was she becoming since spending time with Cifer?

It didn't matter. It was over. No matter how long they spent on the ship together, she wouldn't break again. Work would fill the hole in her chest. That was how she'd gotten over Varik, and it would work with Cifer too.

She made quick work of changing her clothes and repacking her bag. Better to stay on the ship until they left Din' Gale. Something about the beautiful landscapes, rich accommodations, and lack of tasks led her to make impulsive decisions like kissing Cifer. She swiped the back of her hand across her traitorous lips, grabbed her bag, and marched out of the elegant home. Back to reality.

The hover ride back to *The Treasure* was quick and smooth. If the pilot had any concerns about what she was doing leaving in the dark of night, he kindly didn't express them. He'd probably report to Dez and Cyra, but she didn't care. It would only prove how dedicated she was to being the best engineer possible.

Darkness had settled in the corridors of the ship. Blaize flicked the light on her data pad to low, enough to see without tripping. She went to her quarters and dropped her bag. As she came back out, a pink glow filled the space between her door and Cifer's quarters. The glow seemed to intensify as she palmed her door closed. Whatever. The damn orb wasn't her concern.

Blaize leaned against the back wall of the wide cargo bay. Dez supervised the loading of the perishable goods going with them to Chalcanth. Once they launched and she confirmed all was well with the engines, she'd catch some sleep. She pushed herself upright and went to the bridge to confirm with Rhysa and Bodi that their systems checked out.

"You look like shit." Rhysa tilted her head. "Good sex or no sex?"

"Checks for takeoff are complete. Any systems issues for you, Rhysa, or you, Bodi?"

"No sex," Rhysa declared.

"I'm good." Bodi continued to tap on the keys of her console. "Chalcanth Port Authority is expecting us and has granted preliminary docking permission."

Veda arrived and settled into the empty chair to Blaize's right. "Thanks for the help with the plants, Blaize."

"No problem." It truly hadn't been, despite the fact that Blaize had felt eyes on her the entire time she was in the greenhouse with Veda. Probably a leftover reaction from when Cifer had been hiding on the ship, before they knew he'd stowed away.

Dez and Cyra entered the bridge. Dez settled in the chair behind the launch console first, and Cyra lowered herself onto his lap. Blaize forced herself to face forward, despite the tightness in her thighs and the desire in her core.

"We have clearance to launch," Bodi announced without a glance back.

"Navigation is set. Ready when you are, Captain." Rhysa had spun her chair around to face Cyra and Dez, completely shameless.

Blaize glanced back to catch Cyra rolling her eyes at her navigator as they lifted off the flight deck. The real show wasn't required until they were ready to leave the atmosphere. Blaize couldn't help but side-eye the couple over her shoulder. They rose faster and faster as Dez whispered in Cyra's ear, his arm around her middle and his hand between her legs, hidden under layers of diaphanous fabric. Cyra's breathing increased, her chest heaving. Dez scraped his teeth along her neck. Blaize clutched the armrests of her chair as Cyra slammed her hands to the console and released a shuddering moan. *The Treasure* burst through the atmospheric layer and into the dark embrace of space.

Dez scooped Cyra into his arms as he stood. "The captain and I will be in her quarters if needed."

Rhysa let out a joyful whoop.

Blaize squirmed in her chair. The feeling of being watched only made her voyeuristic arousal more embarrassing.

Veda released the straps that held her to the chair. Blaize realized she'd forgotten that critical safety feature.

She followed Veda off the bridge. "I'm going to check the engines."

"Again?" Veda asked.

"Need to make sure I didn't miss anything."

"See you at mid meal," Veda called back before veering into the med bay.

If Blaize forgot something as simple as her safety harness, what else had she missed? She began again from the start and worked her way through each checklist for the third time.

"You still in here?" Veda's voice tore Blaize from staring at the completed list on her pad.

How long had she been staring at the same screen?

"Here." Veda handed her a protein bar. "You missed the meal."

Blaize tugged open the wrapper. If she didn't, the soft-spoken medic would turn fierce and insist on a full medical scan. "Thanks," she said with a full mouth.

"Come on." Veda tugged at Blaize's uniform. "You need to get out of this room. Come breathe some oxygen with me. It's good for the plants."

Blaize let Veda lead her into the greenhouse. And Veda was right. After a few minutes in the greenhouse and finishing the protein bar, she did feel better. Physically.

Silence filled the corners of the room. Veda seemed content to wander from plant to plant, inspecting the small blossoms or emerging fruit. She even had more seedlings started.

"I can't sleep." Blaize clenched her jaw, unsure why she'd admitted the situation to Veda.

"That makes sense. You've been using work to avoid the emotional issue of starting a relationship with Cifer."

Blaize blinked at Veda's back.

"Do you want friendship or a medical opinion on how to get some sleep?"

Blaize wasn't in the frame of mind to dish on her fucked-up relationship—or non-relationship—with Cifer. "Sleep advice?"

"Burn some energy. Get your muscles tired."

"I've been working in the engine room."

Veda shook her head. "Aerobic workout. Either sex or the gym. Equally effective."

"Did you just prescribe sex?"

"It's very effective for insomnia."

Not that Blaize could prove. She hadn't slept well at all since she'd had sex with Cifer. "I think I'll head to the gym."

Veda shrugged. "Okay."

After changing out of her work coveralls, Blaize lingered outside of the room Dez had configured into a gym on the way to Kolben. Workout equipment had been part of his contract to keep him in shape for the mines, but the entire crew made use of it periodically. She didn't hesitate to enter because she was uncertain about working out. It was the voices coming from the room that had her pressing her body against the wall and shifting ever so slowly toward the door while trying to remain unseen.

CHAPTER 27

Cifer resisted the urge to punch the door to his quarters. Blaize was avoiding him again. If he didn't recall how well she kissed him back, he might have believed she didn't want him. But he knew, in his soul, that she wanted him just as badly as he wanted her. For whatever reason, she was denying it, or resisting, or just being stubborn. A hissing growl filled his room.

It was him.

He had to do something to get his emotions under control, or he was going to lose what was left of his mind. Quickly changing into athletic gear, he jogged down the corridors to the workout room. Miles on a treadmill after beating the crap out of a heavy bag might take the edge off. When he arrived, Dez was there, already on a treadmill.

Dez wasn't even panting, though sweat ran thick over his bald head and bare back.

"Could you at least pretend like you're working hard? Ease my poor ego?" Cifer shook his head and looked at the ground as if he were mortified by the other's prowess.

"You require no deception. I've seen you work just as hard." Dez continued to pound a punishing pace on the machine.

Cifer smiled at him, the best smile he could muster under the circumstances, and placed his hands in the glover. The machine laced on the protective gear. He would pretend the body-shaped heavy bag was the male who had hurt Blaize so deeply, she had no trust left.

"Have you secured any of the potential contacts?" Dez asked in a staccato voice that matched his pounding feet.

Cifer released a jab-cross combination on the bag. "Have a couple of bites. Still in negotiations."

Dez groaned. "Why is it always a game? They want the goods. We have the goods."

"The game is the best part," Cifer replied before stepping into the bag and landing an uppercut.

A derisive huff from Dez made Cifer grin.

An hour later, he was panting and lying on the padded floor. A shadow fell over his closed eyes, which he opened to find Dez's concerned face staring down at him, his fists on his hips.

"What troubles you, friend?" Dez asked.

Cifer closed his eyes again.

"Blaize."

Her name falling from the other man's lips was like a needle to his heart—sharp, piercing, fatal. "She hates me."

"You're probably wrong. I thought the same of Cyra. It was fear. Not hate."

"My female is fearless." Cifer rolled and stood. Hearing Dez say she was afraid was an affront to everything Cifer knew about Blaize. She was bold, tireless, selfless, beautiful, giving, sexy, insatiable. And she hated him.

"Your female?" A rumble erupted from the big male's chest that could have been laughter.

"I'm not giving up." Cifer clacked his jaw at Dez, who was taller than him, though not stronger.

"I make no claim on her." Dez held his hand up to show he was unarmed and unwilling to fight.

Some of the tension left Cifer's body. His brain knew that Dez was no threat, happily mated, but his heart, his soul, his entire being needed Blaize to be with him before they would abandon the imaginary battles. "What do I do?"

"You must give her exactly what she needs so that she knows she has nothing to fear from you. So she's sure she can rely on you."

"I don't know what that is."

"Nor do I." Dez chuckled again and slapped Cifer on the shoulder. "But I do know what my mate needs. She's nervous about seeing her family again for the first time since she abandoned their home. I have to be the rock by her side that she can lean against. Let her lead. Trust her enough to follow. Being the mate of a strong, independent female is not an easy path." Dez grinned. "But it's a damn good one." He walked out, leaving Cifer alone in the gym.

Cifer envied the captain. A family reunion of any kind was such a gift, one he'd never get. Dez could easily support Cyra with the task because he had such a great relationship with his own family. He had an example of how families should be. Dez's role in his mate's life was obvious. Unlike Cifer's.

A run might clear his head and let him come up with a plan to give his female exactly what she needed. First, he'd have to figure out where he could fit in her self-driven life.

Despite the long run, Cifer gained no clarity as to what he could do for Blaize, beyond helping her team secure the contracts needed to be successful. At least he could solve the problem of contracting a buyer for the produce on Chalcanth.

He found the communications specialist on the bridge alone.

"Bodi?" he called to her in as soft a voice as he could and still be heard.

She startled, her delicate wings fluttering as she launched herself from her low-backed seat and took a defensive stand. "What are you doing in here?"

"I came to ask you for help, if you would be so kind." He held his arms out from his body, hands low and open.

"You need to run all requests through Captain Cyra or Dez."

"I just came from working out with him." He hadn't asked permission, but that was a minor detail. Dez had assisted with the initial messages, but he had his hands full with his mate. "The only request is to send some more messages. I need to follow up with the buyers for the Din' Gale goods." Among other messages of which Bodi didn't need to know the details.

Cifer took a step, and Bodi bounced back out of reach.

"Why are you terrified of me?" He could have smacked himself. The words were not meant to be vocalized. He waited for her to settle before he moved again.

"Please don't kill me." She held her arms up, defending her face.

"Why would you say that?" He kept his voice soft and his stance as relaxed and as non-threatening as possible.

"There have always been threats on my family's lives. But in the last few months... Blaize says you shouldn't be on this ship."

"I'm sorry. I don't know who you or your family are. Fate is the reason I'm on this ship. Not some nefarious plan. I've never killed anyone in my life." At least not directly. "And I sure don't plan to start, especially with you."

Bodi stared at him for several seconds. She appeared to

weigh his individual atoms and consider their worthiness to be in her presence. "I come from a royal family."

Cifer remained silent.

"I was trained to detect infiltrators and spies."

"Every word I have said to you has been the truth." It was the words he'd omitted that might lead to false assumptions.

"Your words are truthful, but you're cloaked in lies. The contradiction troubles me."

"I'm not a threat."

"But you're hiding something." Her wings moved so quickly, they buzzed.

He held his hands up. "Nothing that could bring harm to you or anyone on this ship."

"Why, then?"

"Habit, mostly. My appearance. It's unusual."

Bodi scanned his body. She gazed into his eyes and nodded solemnly. "What do you need from me?"

"If you could give me some basic instruction on your systems and perhaps a limited account so that I don't have to come to you for every reply and response." Cifer wasn't sure which way it would go. He was certain that Dez would authorize his request, but he didn't want to disturb the male if possible.

"Fine."

Her response surprised and pleased him.

She sat down at the console again and began typing and tapping faster than he could follow. "Your account can be accessed from any console, or you can use your data pad."

"Thank you, Bodi."

"You're going to have to show her. Everything. Before she will trust you."

She was probably right, but once he showed her his true form, there would be no going back. And that was a bridge he couldn't cross—a paradox worse than losing time. If he didn't trust her and show her who he was, he'd lose her, and if he did, the outcome would be the same. He hadn't felt this cold or hopeless since he'd been lying in that ditch on Koblen.

Last meal before they landed on Chalcanth offered another chance to see Blaize. Her voice floated through the corridor, drawing him to the galley. She was laughing with Veda about something that had happened in engineering. Silently, he entered the space, trying not to disrupt her good mood. Blaize was about to take a seat next to Dez. Cifer darted in and blocked the space, clacking his jaw at Dez. Cifer's hand shook as he gestured at the next seat for Blaize to sit.

"What do you think you're doing?" She glared at him but sank into the spot he'd indicated. Her acquiescence calmed him.

He sat next to Dez, who shook his head and chuckled. Cifer looked around the table. All eyes were on them, and every face had a grin. Cifer ducked his head. He didn't know what he was doing, why possessive rage ripped through him, or why he felt challenged by Dez for Blaize's affection. Rational thought had abandoned him.

"Stop that," Blaize hissed at him.

He pulled his hand from her neck, where he'd unconsciously cupped her and was rubbing up and down its length.

Rhysa set a plate in front of him with a knowing grin. "We land in a few hours."

"Cifer? Any progress with the wholesalers?" Dez asked.

"I'll be meeting a buyer at the docks." Cifer tucked into the meal while it was hot. Blaize had nearly finished hers already.

"The docks?" Cyra asked.

"I tried for the spaceport, but apparently the majority of their business is handled on planet between the land masses. So they want to meet at the docks."

"Makes sense." Cyra shrugged and returned to her meal.

The captain seemed to trust him, even if Blaize didn't. He would get the captain the best deal possible to reinforce that trust. Before he could come up with a topic of conversation that included Blaize, she rose from her seat, taking her plate to the sterilizer. "I have some checks to do before we land."

She wasn't talking to him, just making a general announcement before she darted out the door. He could be patient. Maybe. The transaction he was working on would prove how much he cared. Words weren't going to be enough for his beauty.

Once clear of *The Treasure*, in the shadow of a low building close to the docks, Cifer shifted his appearance to that of a Din' Gale native. A breeze wafted over his bare head. He rubbed a gray hand over the exposed skin and tracked the gray stripes along his arm. He resembled the prince more than Dez in size. Not a perfect disguise, but good enough.

He rounded the corner and went to the designated berth where a large sailing ship bobbed in the water. Two males appeared on deck. Both blue-skinned and green-haired, like Captain Cyra...and one too familiar—Varik.

How the fuck had he made it back to his planet of origin? Someone had let this fucker go after he'd purchased children and locked Cifer in a cage. That someone would pay dearly for their corruption.

Cifer adjusted his features to hide his scowl. He had the

advantage, since Varik wouldn't recognize him. First order of business: complete the sale.

Cifer introduced himself as Fursahnd, the name he'd used in the messages.

The captain of the sailing ship gave his name and then turned. "This is my associate, Varik. We'll need to divide the shipment between this ship and his."

"That wasn't our agreement. I have other buyers." Not a lie, but this had been the best price.

The captain sneered. "I'll add a delivery fee to cover your costs. Also, I'll want regular deliveries. I have bratty mouths to feed."

Varik gave a warning grunt.

The back of Cifer's neck prickled. *Bratty mouths to feed* plus Varik. Didn't take a genius to calculate what was happening. "That can be arranged. Where do you need the second delivery?"

"Spaceport."

"Which bay?"

Varik responded with the information and the name of his ship, *Cain's Alibi*.

The Cassan authorities hadn't even confiscated his ship. Someone had been bought off. Cifer filed that away as a future problem. "All right. Give me some time to split the shipment. Equal parts?"

The captain grunted acknowledgement.

"I'll need the payment. First half before I load at the spaceport, and second half when I load here."

"Agreed." The captain held up his data pad, and Cifer transferred payment instructions to his account. Not the original plan. The funds should go to *The Treasure*. But plans had changed.

Cifer kept his disguise in place back at the spaceport. He

had one task to complete before he explained everything to Dez. *Cain's Alibi* was exactly where Varik had said it would be. Cifer slipped into a shadow and shifted his appearance again to blend into the background. With slow, precise movements, he neared the ship and managed to attach the tracker he'd taken with him at the last moment, despite shaking with the recall of the last time he'd been on that ship.

Back at *The Treasure*, Cifer resumed his usual appearance and went to the galley and then the bridge, searching for Dez. He found Veda in Medical. "Have you seen Dez?"

"He's with Cyra. They went to see her family."

Shit. He'd forgotten about that.

"What's wrong?" A wrinkle marred Veda's usually relaxed face.

"Varik is here."

"What?" The screech came from behind him.

Cifer spun to find Blaize in the doorway, glaring.

"Varik's here with the buyer I found for the produce. And I'm concerned about who they're planning to feed."

CHAPTER 28

"What do you mean, Varik's here?" Blaize crossed her arms. "Port authority had him in custody."

Cifer lifted his hands, palms facing her. "It doesn't make any sense to me, either."

"Think about it," Veda's calm voice broke through the tension. "Varik landed a stolen ship in that port. He moved kids into cages under the nose of the port authority."

"He paid them off." Cifer's shoulders dropped. Defeat settled over him, eclipsing his usual energy, and it didn't look right. An urge to comfort him tingled in Blaize's chest.

She'd been blind. He wasn't working with Varik. He cared about the kids. He'd come looking for Dez's help. "Varik's here now. We can't do anything about that." Blaize paused to filter out all her random thoughts and get to the point. "How did he get involved in this trade?"

"I contacted a few people I know who move goods." Cifer huffed out a breath. "It's not something I do a lot. I'm a retriever, not a procurer. I put out feelers to the people they recommended. This captain was the first to respond. Didn't flinch at the price."

"He met you at the docks?" Veda asked.

"Yeah. Said he couldn't leave his ship." Cifer's eyes went wide. "Do you think he's got kids on the ship?"

Veda nodded. "It's possible. Chalcanth has limited resources because so much of the planet is water. They track most purchases to make sure people aren't hoarding or selling items procured at the state stores on the black market."

"Shit." Cifer ran his hand over the back of his neck. "Was I supposed to go through government channels? No one said."

Veda shook her head. "Off-planet goods aren't regulated like that. I mean, they'll want their cut."

"How do you know so much about this, Veda?" Blaize asked.

Veda's dark cheeks reddened. "I looked into what I could do with the produce I'm growing in case I had too much and we couldn't eat it all. It's not been a problem, but I had imagined unprecedented success. I knew we'd be coming to Cyra's planet, so I checked the rules."

"What do we do?" Cifer asked.

"We could wait for Dez and Cyra," Veda replied.

"No." Blaize couldn't stand the idea of another group of kids being caught in Varik's web. How the fuck did the fucker get his hands on so many babies? And why?

"I think I know why," Cifer answered.

Had she said that out loud? "Explain."

"Pretty sure the situation on Cassan was an opportunity that presented itself. Varik's obviously got a problem with Captain Cyra, *The Treasure*, and you." His gaze was pointed, and Blaize dropped her gaze, still embarrassed to have been intimate with such an ass. "He saw how upset you were by the kids being taken. He likely also had a big credit investment in the purchase, and you ruined that for him."

"Me? What about you?"

"I was locked in the cage, remember?"

She couldn't forget. Cifer incapacitated, caged like an animal. "We should notify the authorities."

"And tell them what?" Cifer asked. "That some guys want to buy some produce we're trying to sell?"

Blaize frowned. "We have to do something."

"Maybe we should wait for Cyra and Dez." Veda twisted her fingers together.

"What if they leave before we can do anything?" Blaize didn't believe waiting was the right answer. The situation required action. If only she knew what action. She didn't have a checklist for rescuing abducted kids, having only done it once before. "If this keeps happening, I'm going to need an SOP and a checklist."

"SOP?" Cifer's wrinkled brow was kind of adorable.

"Standard operating procedure." How could anyone not know that?

"I don't think there's a standard procedure for retrieving people or objects that have been stolen. It's more of a respond-in-the-moment kind of situation."

Blaize clenched her jaw. There had to be best practices. Maybe she could do a search and get advice. Write down her takeaways from the previous event and lessons learned from this one, assuming Varik had abducted kids again. And that she and Cifer could free them.

"It's more important to know your own capabilities. Trust your instincts and be ready to respond to the unexpected."

She'd avoided the unexpected as much as possible for most of her life. Danger filled the gaps around the unexpected.

"We just need to decide what the next step is," Cifer said.

"Keep them from taking the kids." That was obvious.

"And how are we going to do that?" Cifer's tone was calm and respectful.

"Keep the ship from leaving. But you don't think the authorities will help." What other option was there?

"They probably would if we could prove our assumption. But we can't."

Blaize pursed her lips. There were lots of ways to keep a ship from flying. "I need to know the class, manufacturer, and model of the ship. If I have that, I can get the schematics and figure out what part to remove or sabotage to keep Varik from taking off. But even if I had that, I'm not sure how we could execute the modification. Most of the critical parts are deep inside, and you have to get on the ship to access those sensitive areas. It seems like a long shot." Not to mention totally illegal, but so was stealing kids.

"I'll get you the exact information you need. Give me an hour. In the meantime, get some rest. We'll need the cover of night to hide this gorgeous flame." Cifer ran his fingers through a tendril of her hair. His gaze was filled with admiration and longing.

She'd missed him. Anger and hurt had masked the longing, but over the past few cycles, the mask had lifted. The shiver that went through her at his nearness had nothing to do with anger. "I'll, uh, go. Now. Rest. Like you said. Get me as soon as you have the information."

"Okay, Beauty."

Blaize glanced at Veda, whose smile was so big it made her eyes crinkle. Heat bloomed over Blaize's face, and she darted out of the sick bay and back toward her room. A pink glow filled the hallway, and even though she shouldn't, she crept into Cifer's room, drawn to the source of the light.

Pink illumination filled the room, making everything appear soft and inviting, especially Cifer's bed. Was his bed nicer than the one she had in her quarters? She pressed a hand to the mattress. Maybe a little softer. She sat. Not too soft. She kicked off her boots and laid out. The mattress hugged her. His scent on the pillow reminded her how well she'd slept in his bed on Cassan. She closed her eyes and breathed him in, letting herself revel in the reminder of the night they'd shared. Her anger at him made no sense. Not there in his room, bathed in the pink light and cradled in his bed. In a few minutes, she'd get up and leave. Go back to her own quarters. She curled around and hugged his pillow. Soon, but not yet.

Cifer raced back to *The Treasure*, pausing only to revert his blue skin back to the coppery color he normally used. The mission to gather the data Blaize needed had been a success. He'd even managed to get a serial number. Silent emptiness greeted him as he entered the ship that had started to feel like home. He checked the galley. No one there. No one on the bridge. No one in medical. Veda rarely left the ship. She was probably in the greenhouse. But she wasn't the person he searched for. *Blaize*. Had she taken his advice and rested, or was she crawling around the engine room with a checklist in one hand? He glanced at the corridor to the quarters and turned toward the cargo bay.

The engine room was completely silent. If Blaize was in there, she'd be talking to the machinery. He retraced his steps and proceeded down the hall to her door. Before he got there, pink light streamed into the hall from the vents and micro-openings around his door. That wasn't fucking normal. What the hell was going on with the orb?

He smacked the panel that controlled his door, and as it slid open, a breathtaking vision met him. Red hair splayed over his pillow. His woman curled in his bed. The lighting made her seem ethereal. She moaned, and Cifer entered his room, closing the door behind him.

"Cifer." Her body undulated in a sensual move that made his cock stiffen. Her hand twisted between her legs.

He leaned back against the door. He shouldn't be watching her like this, but he couldn't look away, and she was in *his* room, calling *his* name.

"Yes." The word wrapped itself around him, tugging him forward, but he resisted. She didn't know he was there.

She shuddered, and the move shook him. The sensation of her fluttering around his cock was as unmistakable as it was unbelievable. Whatever the orb was doing to them, he had to lock it down before the entire ship fell under the spell. He shot his arms to the vent cover and removed the plate.

"What are you doing? How's it possible for your arm to stretch like that?"

Cifer craned his neck to peer at the beauty who was sitting up in his bed, wide-eyed and open-mouthed. He grabbed the orb with one hand and replaced the vent cover with the other. "I need to lock this up somewhere safer."

She popped out of his bed, her cheeks as red as her mane. "I shouldn't be in here."

"I disagree. This is exactly where you should be. Every night."

Blaize shook her head, ran her fingers through her hair. The orb glowed brighter, like it was on fire. "I saw the light in the hall, and... I'm sorry. I came in uninvited. I know that's against the rules of polite society and probably against the captain's rules for privacy, but I couldn't resist. And then I was so tired. I didn't mean to fall asleep. It was just so relaxing and inviting... I should go."

She darted forward, and he held out an arm, tugging her to him. "Don't go." He rubbed his cheek against her soft, pale skin.

She melted into him for the briefest moment. A taste of paradise.

With a jolt backwards, she stiffened. "What about the kids? Did you get the information?"

Cifer pressed his lips tight. The orb dimmed. "I did."

"Really?"

"Let me lock this up with Veda." She had to have some kind of medical waste container that could hold the damn glowing rock. "Then we'll make a plan."

She pressed her lips to his. Her unexpected move was over before he could respond. The door slid open at her command, and she darted out into the hallway. "See you on the bridge."

Cifer wobbled in place. She'd kissed him. Willingly. Initiated the connection. His heart glowed brighter than the orb. He had a chance.

But first, they had to stop Varik.

CHAPTER 29

Blaize pressed her fingers to her lips as she rushed to the bridge. She couldn't outrun the impulse or the dream she had. In. His. Bed. Another wave of heat flooded her. She should be freaked out by the way his arms had stretched unnaturally to retrieve the orb. But all the skills he had—the ability to change his appearance—only intrigued her. She'd have given anything to change her appearance as a child to blend with the members of her community. But the more time she spent on *The Treasure,* and with Cifer, the less she worried about how she looked. No one teased her about being translucent or a moon rock or a demon. She was just Blaize. Engineer. Desirable.

That last one was the most difficult to resolve. Cifer desired her. As much control as he had over his body, he couldn't hide the way he reacted. He was authentically attracted to her. But her fascination with the man would have to wait until they could once again deal with the vile pest that kept reappearing.

She took her usual seat on the bridge and logged into the ship's computer. Before she could decide her first move, Dez and Cyra arrived.

"Captain." Blaize stood. Cyra looked more relaxed than Blaize had ever seen her. "It looks like you had a good visit with your family, but I'm sorry... There's been an unexpected development. Cifer had a buyer for the Din' Gale shipment, like he told you, but then he found out the male was working with Varik. Varik's here, on Chalcanth. And we think he might have more kids. So, we're going to try to stop him. Cifer got the information about the ship. I think I can find a way to disable it so Varik can't get away again before we get proof. And hopefully, there are some decent law-abiding officers here who will keep him in custody instead of accepting a bribe to let him go." Blaize sucked in a breath.

Rhysa entered the bridge before Dez or Cyra could respond. Her hair was messy, and her clothes were wrinkled. She wore a huge smile. "What's going on?"

"Varik is on planet," Dez replied.

Rhysa halted mid-saunter. "He's an unsquishable bug. What are we doing about it?"

Blaize appreciated that Rhysa aligned instantly about dealing with the problem.

"I'm not sure there's much we can do." Cyra's gills flapped. "If the Cassan authorities didn't keep him—"

"He's got more kids. I'm sure of it." Cifer went to Blaize and stood facing Dez and the captain. "They were buying the food. All of it. We know Varik only has one other crew member. The sailing ship of the buyer was big, but there were very few crew members when we met."

"Blaize, you have a plan?" Cyra asked.

"Yes, Captain." Blaize took a breath. "Cifer should find another buyer while I research Varik's spaceship. We need to incapacitate it so he can't leave with the kids."

Silence lingered, and Blaize pressed her lips together. She didn't have to fill it.

Dez crossed his arms. "What about the other ship? The watercraft."

"I— I don't know." Blaize winced at the hole in the plan Dez had so quickly identified.

"My brother works security at the docks. Just started there." The pride in Cyra's voice was clear. Blaize hadn't known the captain had a sibling.

Dez nodded. "We'll contact him. Blaize can figure out what to do about Varik's ship. I'd rather we contacted the port authority here, but that didn't work out last time. So, let's find the right people to handle this."

Bodi rushed in with a large bag in each hand. She paused at the entrance, just inside the bridge. "What's going on? Where's Veda? I found the perfect thing for her."

Rhysa spun in her chair. "You went shopping?"

Bodi scowled back at her. "Chalcanth fabrics are universally famous. You could have come with me instead of getting fucked by strangers."

"I'm sure that, as much as you paid for whatever is in those two sacks, we both got screwed."

Blaize blocked out the rest of the conversation and began the search for the ship schematics. Bodi and Rhysa would get tired of their toxic banter, and nothing she could say would help. Dez and Cyra left the bridge. Cifer settled into the empty chair next to her and tapped away. Hopefully, one of his other contacts would come through and they could offload the produce. Worst case, they'd eat really well on the way to Hiargus.

But first, the problem of disabling Varik's ship. Blaize entered the information Cifer had gathered. *There.* The class, make, and model of the ship piloted by Varik. She added the serial number but didn't have the date of manufacture. That last detail, and she'd be completely certain that she had the right plans, but as it was, she was ninety-eight percent sure. If she could read the digital identification... But no way Varik left the DID untampered. She clicked through the screens, focusing on the external panels and the mechanics behind them.

"This could work."

"What?" Cifer crouched by her side, one arm around her chair.

She hadn't meant to say that out loud, not until she verified. But since he was already there... "See? This panel. If we can get it open, and if I have the right tool to reach back to there..." She pointed at the screen as she zoomed in on the schematic.

"I'm pretty sure I'll be able to reach it." He gave her a half-smile.

"That connector provides the power connection to the nav system. If that were to *come loose*, the ship won't launch. It's in the safety checks. No nav system verification, no liftoff."

Cifer kissed her cheek. "Brilliant." He stood up before she could react to either. "I'll go tonight."

"*We'll* go tonight." She touched his arm to get his attention. "You need my expertise."

Cifer opened his mouth. Clamped his jaw shut. Crossed his arms and glared at her. "Fine. But you have to do everything I say. I won't have you get caught by the bastards."

"Like you were?" Blaize couldn't believe she'd said that. "I... Um... I didn't—"

"Yes, Beauty. Like I was. I don't think I could stand to see you in a cage." He caressed her shoulder.

Warm, gooey affection shoved Blaize's embarrassment away.

"Ah, true love." Rhysa smirked at Blaize.

Cifer tugged the hood of the jacket tight over Blaize's head and tucked each stray lock of her gorgeous red hair away. "You'll listen to me. Do everything when I say. Nothing else, and not until I say so."

"I know what I'm doing."

Her lip stuck out adorably, and he considered kissing her silly, fucking her senseless, and leaving her safely behind. "You know what you're doing with the engines. But you don't have a clue about breaking the rules and stealth missions."

"I saved you, didn't I?"

Cifer tilted his head. "You beat the hell out of a ship with a giant wrench and then broke open cages with the same blunt force tool. Not stealthy."

"Fine." She stepped out of his reach. "I'll let you lead."

He tugged her forward and gave her a quick kiss. "You can lead later."

A calculated look flashed across her face, and Cifer couldn't wait to find out what she had in mind. But first they had to deal with that bastard, Varik.

In the loading bay, Rhysa leaned against the wall next to the door. "I'm going with."

She was dressed all in black and stood as Cifer and Blaize approached. Cifer scowled. "This isn't a party."

"I'd be dressed differently if it was," Rhysa shot back. "You two will be busy with the ship. I'll keep watch."

Cifer considered the change in plan. Not a terrible idea to have some backup.

"Dez suggested I tag along. He and Cyra are meeting her brother at the shipyards." Rhysa's pink-eyed gaze narrowed. "By suggested, I mean ordered."

"Fine. But same rules apply. You do what I say and only what I say when I tell you."

She rolled her eyes. "Duh."

Cifer already regretted agreeing to her coming, and they hadn't even left.

Using the shadows of the other ships, Cifer led the two women toward *Cain's Alibi*. The smaller ship was at the opposite end of the port from *The Treasure*. Cifer had noted the cameras, and while the coverage was good, it wasn't perfect. Cameras were more of a deterrent and after-the-fact evidence than any kind of warning system. He would not be deterred when it came to protecting kids, and if the mission went according to plan, no one would need to review the images for evidence. He slowed as they neared the target ship. The splash of water at the edges of the tarmac covered any sounds they created but made confirming no one was around more challenging.

"Wait here. I'll get the panel off, and then I'll signal like we practiced."

Rhysa melted into the shadows.

Blaize handed him a slim metal tool. "You'll need this for the bolts."

He took the tool, even though it was unnecessary. His ability to morph his body meant tools were always at his fingertips. "Stay."

The panel came off easily enough. Before he could wave her over, Blaize was at his side. She shone a flashlight into the cavity. Wires going every which way, multiple flexible conduits, and pipes filled the tight space.

"That one." Blaize pointed with her finger and the flashlight.

Cifer handed her the tool and stretched his arm into the cramped space.

"No, to the left."

Footsteps stomped down a ramp.

"Hurry," Blaize urged.

Rhysa's voice wafted to them from under the ship. Was she trying to provide a distraction? Had they been found out?

Cifer tugged on the connector, but it was stuck.

"What the fuck do you think you're doing?"

He yanked harder. The connector popped free. Cifer snatched the flashlight out of Blaize's hand and shone it in the face of the confronter. "Run," he hissed at Blaize. "Get Dez. Run."

"Get that fucking light out of my eyes. Who are you? What are you doing to my ship?"

"Go. Now." Every instinct screamed at Cifer himself to run. He could get out of the situation, but not with Blaize at risk.

Blaize crept away from him, and as soon as she was in the shadows, her heavy footfalls testified to her obedience. Floodlights on vehicles lit the area. Blaize screeched. Varik suckerpunched Cifer, and he dropped the flashlight. A port officer came around the ship a moment later. Cifer could still escape, but they had Blaize. He raised his hands in surrender.

Varik laughed. "Got you."

The officers put Cifer in the same vehicle as Blaize. She leaned toward the barrier between the driver and the containment portion of the vehicle—a box with staggered benches. "You don't understand. We're the good guys. That ship is being used to traffic children. All you have to do is go in there. He has cages. There will be kids in those cages. You have to believe me. Please check. You'll never forgive yourself if I'm right and you find out too late. They could be kids of people you know."

Cifer had to give it to Blaize. Her emotional appeal was on point, but she'd killed any argument he could make that she wasn't involved. He'd already freed himself from the shackles. The officer eyeballed Blaize.

"Please, I'm not lying. You have to check."

As soon as the uniformed male left the vehicle, Cifer released Blaize's cuffs.

"What are you doing?"

"Getting you out of here. They don't need us both. They can blame me."

"If you can get *me* out, you can leave too. Come with me." Blaize tugged on his arm even as she shifted one leg out the door he'd opened.

"That won't work, Beauty. They have to have someone in custody. Otherwise, they'll hunt us down, and the entire crew would be compromised." He pressed his lips to hers, savoring their last kiss. "Deliver the orb. Collect the fee." His future didn't matter. Only hers. Blaize's safety mattered more than anything else.

"What about the kids?"

"If they're on this ship, they'll find them." He nudged her. "Go, now. While you can."

She glanced back a few steps into her escape. He jutted his chin for her to continue, his hands back in the cuffs. He'd sworn he'd never sacrifice his freedom, his reputation, or his income for another being. But that was before he fell in love. There was something fitting about having to give her up and take the blame, considering everything he'd gotten away with in his life. But his heart still ached with her absence.

CHAPTER 30

Blaize raced back to *The Treasure*, Rhysa at her side. She wasn't leaving Cifer.

The ramp was down. Veda and Bodi stood at the top of the stairs.

"Where's Cifer?" Veda asked before Blaize had even cleared the ramp.

"Back of a patrol unit last we saw," Rhysa answered.

"He insisted I leave." Tears stung Blaize's eyes. "He said we should launch. Deliver the orb without him." She sniffed and moved past the group toward the bridge. "I'm not leaving him on Chalcanth."

"What do you mean, he insisted you leave?" Bodi asked, close on Blaize's heels.

"I was arrested too, and he got me out of the restraints and opened the door so I could go." She picked up the pace to jog down the corridor. "He sacrificed himself, but that doesn't work for me." She slammed to stop at the entrance to the bridge. "Where's the captain?"

"Here." Cyra's voice echoed in the corridor behind her.

Blaize spun on her heel. "We have to get him back."

"Who?" Cyra asked.

"Cifer." Blaize searched for the words to explain. She opened her mouth, and the words poured out.

Cyra glanced at Dez. He nodded as if she'd given her mate instructions. "We'll get him back."

Blaize took a full breath. If Dez said it and the captain ordered it, Cifer would be freed. "How?"

"We had a bit more success than you did." Cyra placed her hand on Dez's arm. "Dez found the secret compartment on the ship where they were holding the kids. They're being reunited with their parents as soon as arrangements can be made. The captain and several of the crew are in custody. All we have to do is go to the authorities and explain that Varik was in league with the operation."

Blaize admired and respected Captain Cyra, but Varik was a slippery bastard. If there was a way to evade responsibility for his actions, he was already working on it. "We should go now. To the authorities. What if they didn't search Varik's ship? He could get away with other kids."

"You said you pulled the connector?" Cyra asked.

"Yeah, but that's a five-minute fix."

"I'll go," Dez said.

"I'm going with you." Blaize crossed her arms.

"We're all going." Cyra was flanked by Veda, Bodi, and Rhysa. "We don't leave a team member behind." She squeezed Dez's hand, and he gave her the most loving look.

Blaize sucked in her lip as tears threatened to fall again. Cifer was part of the team, even if he didn't know it yet.

Cifer belonged on *The Treasure*.

Cifer gripped the bars of the cell he'd been placed in to keep from pacing. For a person who prided themselves on never getting caught, he was having an extremely bad run. He cocked his head to listen more carefully. He could have sworn Blaize was in the building, but that was impossible. She'd been running back to *The Treasure* last he saw her. His heart pounded in his chest, and the urge to break out rode him hard. But if he escaped, Blaize would be at risk. He clenched the bars so hard his fingers ached.

Moments later, an officer opened the door and walked in, followed by Dez. Cifer had never been so overjoyed to see another male. Voices from the offices trailed through the opening. Blaize was there—with the entire team, if his ears didn't deceive him.

"Furcifer Msuya, you're free to go." The officer placed her palm on the biometric pad, and the cage clicked open.

Cifer didn't question the officer. He didn't need answers. He needed freedom. And he was so grateful that they hadn't left him behind. As soon as he stepped out and breathed the air outside the cage, which was logically the exact same as the air inside but somehow tasted sweeter, his muscles softened and his lungs inflated a bit more. "Where's Blaize? Is she okay?"

Cifer had many more questions, but not until they were away from the authorities who had locked him up. Dez didn't respond. Cifer followed the gray male to the lobby where the rest of the crew waited, including the fiery, beautiful woman who had stolen his heart.

"Blaize." Her name whispered from his lips like a prayer of thanks, a promise, and a plea.

She launched herself into his waiting arms and answered all of his needs with a single word. "Cifer."

He clenched her close and buried his face in her hair, breathing her in. Her clean scent was his new definition of home. Too soon, she stepped out of his embrace and clasped his hand.

They were surrounded by the smiling faces of the crew of *The Treasure*.

"What about the kids?" Cifer demanded.

"All safe and sound, thanks to you." Blaize squeezed his hand.

"Let's go home," Cyra said.

The female meant her ship. The crew's ship. Blaize's home.

The only home he'd ever dreamed of was on a planet that was no longer reachable with current technology.

Dez invited him into the galley while the rest of the crew prepped for launch.

Cifer queried Blaize with a look.

"I'll be in the engine room. Come find me when you're done."

He reluctantly released her hand and stared as she walked off in the opposite direction.

"Come on. She's not going anywhere without you."

Dez's words calmed Cifer enough that he could take his eyes off her and go to the galley. At least for a few minutes.

After he got them each a cold fermented beverage, Dez sat at the table. Cifer took the silent invitation and settled into a chair, nervous about what Dez would say.

"So, I know you have tremendous skills and are contracted for exorbitant rates."

Cifer wasn't sure how Dez knew that but nodded.

"Veda tells me the orb is locked up in her med lab."

Cifer nodded again, not sure how the two topics went together.

"Our next stop is Hiargus, so you can get paid and get that

thing off our ship." Dez took a long drink of the brew. "You have any other jobs lined up?"

Cifer hesitated, unused to discussing his business with anyone else. But Dez represented the family he wanted. "Actually, no. The payout for the orb would be enough to keep me and the orphanage funded for a galactic year. I planned to take some time and be selective."

Dez nodded and took another sip of the brew. Silence didn't make Cifer antsy, so he let the male take his time in responding, even though the urge to find Blaize rode him hard.

"Would you consider staying on?"

"Staying on *The Treasure*?" With Blaize?

"I've been filling the role of Chief of Security *and* negotiating our jobs. You are a much better negotiator."

Cifer jolted back. "Not sure how you can say that when the first group I negotiated with wanted the food from Din' Gale to feed stolen kids."

"The backup buyer you had in place was more than ready to take the goods." Dez's yellow-eyed gaze lasered into Cifer. "You did the work to have two buyers set up. Probably three if I checked. I struggle to negotiate a single deal. To be honest, I hate it. I've learned two things trying to fill that role. Not everyone is as honest as the Din' Gale people. And two, I don't like to dicker."

"It's a game." Cifer shrugged. "Played correctly, everyone wins."

"So, will you do it? Will you join *The Treasure*?"

"What does Blaize think of all this?"

"She thinks..."

Cifer twisted in his seat. Blaize was in the doorway, stealing his breath, which only made sense since she already had his heart.

She continued, "She would very much like you to stay and

be a partner. The entire team discussed it, and the vote was unanimous to make you a partner. But if you don't want to stay, obviously we would still meet the terms of the agreement we came to on Cassan and take you to Hiargus and then back to Cassan. No one is kidnapping you or forcing you to—"

Cifer stretched out an arm and tugged her close, kissing her rambling mouth. In a perfect world, he'd respectfully wait for her to finish. But neither the world, nor he, was perfect, and he couldn't wait a moment longer.

She gasped for breath. "Is that a yes?"

"There could be no other answer to such an invitation. I'll sign whatever contract you need. After."

"After?" Blaize asked.

"After we launch and I take you back to your quarters—or mine—and seal this partnership properly."

"Okay," Blaize replied, her cheeks pink and her gaze dreamy.

"See? Expert negotiator," Dez said, rising from his chair.

"Everyone gets what they want." Cifer tugged Blaize behind him to the bridge. The sooner they launched, the sooner he could get her in his bed.

CHAPTER 31

BLAIZE CLOSED the door to her quarters. The launch had been perfect, and the team was relieved to have Cifer as their new partner. No one liked to negotiate, except for Rhysa, and her version of negotiation had a limited audience.

"Come here, Beauty." Cifer gripped her hand, pulling her away from the door.

"Wait."

Cifer released her, his face a mask of confusion. And that was the final hurdle—his infinite masks.

"I need you to do something for me before we go any further."

He grinned. "Anything."

"I want to see you. No illusions. Just you as you are."

His grin faded. "You might not like what you see."

"I love you. I'll love what I see."

"I love you, too."

"I want more than your love. I want your trust." And by giving her his trust, he'd be gaining hers, whether he knew it or not.

Cifer tugged his shirt up and over his head. Blaize traced

the shadows of his muscles with her gaze. Cifer raised an eyebrow. "What if I'm fat and out of shape?"

"I've seen you work out with Dez. Pretty sure those muscles aren't an illusion. And even if they were, it's not just your body I'm attracted to. Your heart. The way you care for kids. Your honorable side. That's what has me quaking every time I see you. That's what convinced me to look beyond the seeming betrayal of you leaving and to examine all your actions as a whole. You might break the rules, but you have good reasons."

"So, I'm an honorable thief now?" He released the clasp on his pants.

Blaize lost the ability to form words as he slowly exposed his hard cock. She wasn't so dumb as to not hope that his cock remained largely the same. Emphasis on largely. Her cheeks heated.

"I'd love to know what thought put that color on your face, Beauty."

"You're stalling."

"You can't unsee me once I show you."

She leaned against the wall as if she wasn't a massive ball of tension. "Anytime now."

He kicked off his boots and shed his pants. Naked but not real. Not yet.

She swallowed and remembered to blink.

"Ready?"

She nodded.

His body seemed to shimmer and stretch, much like when he'd reached into the panel on Varik's ship or into the vent to retrieve the orb. Except more than his arm shifted. His skin became noticeably greener. His hair retreated to a short covering of his scalp. The outlines of scales appeared around his shoulders, hips, and feet. He seemed shorter, closer to her height. But she'd been right. His muscles were still there, even more prominent. She straightened from her relaxed stance as an appendage appeared from behind his hips. A thick, muscular tail, wide at the base, narrowing to a tip no larger than his thumb.

"I knew it," she gasped.

"What?" His startled tone and step back had her rushing to embrace him.

"Knew you'd be gorgeous. Knew your muscles were real." She grinned up at him. "Knew you had a tail."

"How?"

"You may not have been aware of it, but this extra appendage..." She reached around him and stroked her hand over the base of his tail where it met his ass, stealing his breath. "It made an appearance the night we made love."

A reddish hue tinted his green cheeks. "I've never lost control like that before."

"Until now."

"Now?"

Blaize released the clasps on her boots and freed her feet. Her coveralls were next. Cifer stared at her plain bra and panties as if they were the finest lace spun by Aranidot weavers. He reached out a hand and hesitated.

"Touch me." The words barely cleared her lips before she was enveloped in his embrace, his mouth on her neck, her shoulders, her lips. She ran her hands over his body too, learning him anew. The scales on his shoulders weren't rough. Like a callus more than a sharp edge. She liked the contrast of the roughness to the smooth flesh that covered the rest of his body.

He slid a finger inside her opening. "So wet and hot."

"For you." She shuddered as he slid in a second finger and pumped them, preparing her for what she hungered for. The moan that escaped her lips when he left her body carried the weight of her need for him.

"I can't wait."

She caressed his face. "I don't want you to wait."

"I've got you." Cifer cradled her upper body in his arms. His tail took control of her leg, lifting and spreading her open. He bent his knees and notched the head of his cock at her opening.

"Fucking talented," she breathed.

"I can shift my cock into any shape you like." The tentative tone in his voice pricked her heart.

"No. You. As you are. I want the real us." She pressed her lips to his.

He thrust up. She went to her tiptoes and lost her breath as he stretched and filled her, lifting her completely off her feet and sliding her down his cock. Strong, thick, flexible, and so much more—his body was a universe all by itself. One she'd never finish exploring.

He took a few steps, each move resonating through her core, making his cock drill deeper. She squeezed her eyes shut, focusing completely on how he filled and stretched her so perfectly. He pressed her against the wall of her room, the cold a sharp contrast to his heat. Sensations washed over her faster than she could process. He bent his head, thrust out his tongue, and extended it to lash her nipple. She clenched as the sensation registered so much lower. "Oh damn, that's a fucking skill."

He leaned back and laughed. "Literally."

"We're exploring that talent again. In a bed."

He dipped his knees to thrust up and into her with committed force. "We'll explore everything, Beauty. All the positions, all the places, all the ways I can make you come."

And she was on the edge of doing exactly that, her body sensitive and shaking, her pussy weeping over his cock as he slid in and out, each time going seemingly deeper. Who knows. Maybe he was. Whatever he was doing, he should keep doing it. Because—

The tip of his tail teased between her cheeks, tickling her sensitive, untried ring.

She exploded. Like a rocket firing for launch, her entire body responded to the detonation that started in her core. She bathed him in her cum, breath heaved from her lungs in a scream, and her muscles went rigid. Through it all, he held her in place, continued to pump in and out, his green-eyed gaze pouring passion into her. She couldn't control her head falling back and her eyes closing as the power of the moment washed through her with aftershocks.

And then, he followed her into space, his body going rigid, his grip tightening. The idea of his prints on her thighs made her body clench around his, and he roared, his rhythm gone and his cock juddering inside her. She ignited again as he rocked into her, taking her deeper into a space only the two of them could be, the space and the stars they'd created with their explosive connection.

She dropped her head onto his shoulder, completely spent. His rich scent filled her lungs, bringing a sense of belonging deep into her soul. It was an unfamiliar sensation she'd spend a lifetime getting used to. He lowered her onto the bed and left her body. She moaned at the loss.

"Be right back." He kissed her forehead and freed himself from her embrace.

Blaize's gaze was drawn to him. Muscles rippled down his back. Two taught globes framed his thick tail that didn't quite reach the ground before it tapered to a point. She'd never been with a male with extra appendages. Gills had been the most exotic, but Cifer's appearance didn't seem exotic. He was as he should be. His true form made sense. He shouldn't have to hide.

"You have a choice," he said when he returned from the bathroom. "This or my tongue?" He held up a damp cloth.

"That's a question?"

Cifer laughed, stretched his arm back to the bath to drop the towel, and then settled between her legs. "Get comfortable, Beauty. I'm going to be very, very thorough."

"Nice trick. With the towel."

"I know a lot more tricks." He gave her a wicked grin and extended his tongue.

She squirmed, and he held her in place as he took her over the edge again and again.

Banging on the door woke Cifer. He shifted his appearance and quickly put on his pants. Rhysa was on the other side of the door, a huge grin plastered on her face. She attempted to peer around him.

He shifted his body to close the gaps. "What's up?"

"Dez cooked. Sent me to collect you two since Blaize isn't answering her comm. Did you put her in a coma?"

Part of him wanted to puff out his chest and assure her that he had treated Blaize very well. "We'll be there momentarily."

"Good. It's tradition for the crew to eat together after we launch. Family style."

"Give me just a minute," Blaize called from behind him. "But don't wait for us. I'm sorry I missed the call. I don't know what came over me. I—"

"I'm pretty sure I know what came over you, in you, and all the other ways you can come. Good for you, Blaize. But hurry up. I'm hungry." Rhysa spun on her heel, her laughter echoing behind her.

Cifer struggled to dress, distracted by the pale, pristine perfection that was his beauty. Blaize managed to finish cleaning up and securing her clothing before him, despite his head start. He shoved his feet into his boots and clasped her hand, enjoying the simple walk to the galley.

Two empty chairs waited for them. Bowls of steaming food filled the table, and the entire crew's gaze locked on him and his lover. He held down the proud smile and tried not to puff out his chest too far. Pride didn't begin to capture how he felt about his relationship. And then there was the warm, soft sensation of being surrounded by the crew. Embraced into the fold of their unity. He hadn't belonged on *The Treasure* when he first stepped on board. Yet, after such a short time, he couldn't imagine belonging anywhere else.

Bowls passed from hand to hand, food scooped out onto their plates. Rhysa's voice carried over the polite pleases and thank-yous. "We're set for Hiargus. I found the best route, but it will still take months."

Cyra held the platter of meat for Dez. "Shouldn't be a problem. We have plenty of food and fuel."

"Not a problem for you or Blaize," Rhysa replied. "I hope I brought enough batteries."

Bodi laughed. "There's always fingers."

"Yours or mine?" Rhysa asked.

Bodi rolled her eyes. "Never gonna happen."

"Aw, Princess. I'm so disappointed." Rhysa stuck out her tongue.

Bodi shifted her shoulder and gave Rhysa an imperious smile. "You couldn't handle me."

Veda laughed so hard, she slipped off her chair.

Blaize squeezed Cifer's hand, and he met her gaze with a smile. She mouthed a single, perfect, once-unattainable word. *Family.*

CHAPTER 32

Varik keyed in the navigation to Cassan with a shaky hand. It wasn't his strong suit, but he knew enough to get hired onto the shuttle transport. After months in lockup while he waited for his lawyer to work through the hearings, any job on any ship going anywhere would have been welcome. Especially after seeing what the legal system had done to Karnek.

The judge's proclamation had been on all the streams. "Karnek Hastalik, you are nearby sentenced to twenty galactic years in prison, or you may choose to serve your time on Kolben for no more than ten years."

His former communication specialist had to write down his response, due to his jaw still being wired shut. Varik couldn't blame him for not taking the Kolben option. Not that twenty years on the notorious prison moon circling Morgual was much better. But at least there was at least a chance he'd live.

Varik had served three galactic months in community service to his planet for being an accessory to child endangerment and forfeited his ship. Technically, Karnek lost the ship, since it had been in his name. All of it supported Varik's claim that he'd known nothing about the children on the ship and that it was all Karnek's doing.

"Varik, have you set the course?"

Varik gritted his teeth. "Aye, Captain."

"Let's get underway." The captain relaxed into his chair as if it were a throne and not a worn-out, cracked polymer seat on a basic transport shuttle.

They carried a total of thirty-six passengers and five crew, plus the captain. There were no quarters, only reclining seats. The shuttle was a bare-bones solution for the poor workers who traveled to or from Cassan. The lack of frills and accommodations was one reason Varik had been able to get the job, but he wouldn't be keeping it.

As soon as they landed, he'd be able to reconnect with some of the former crew from *The Treasure* to secure a new job, maybe a new ship, and possibly a new identity. He had the credits in his secret, secure account.

Varik barely slept the entire trip to Cassan. Once they docked, he stood and stretched, his back cracking and muscles aching.

"You have one-cycle leave. Report back here at six. System checks and passenger load will start shortly after." The hair on the captain's lip fluttered with each word.

Varik resisted the urge to rip it from his face. There was no fucking way he'd ever get back on the low-budget shuttle. "Aye, Captain."

He couldn't quit. It was part of the conditions of his release that he keep a job. But good luck to the Chalcanth officials ever finding Varik again. The time had come to restart with a new identity. But first, he needed a shower, a meal, and a fuck.

With the only credits in his active account those the shuttle company had deposited, he avoided the hired sled and marched down to the subfloor trams. Being surrounded by more low-budget travelers only reinforced his decision to disappear with the credits he had remaining from his dead lover and former captain, Auvi.

The rented room opened to his code. He breathed a sigh of relief and ignored the fine layer of dust over every surface. After he showered, he ordered food and a fuck. He didn't care which got there first.

He slumped into the only chair in the room, his wet towel around his hips, and closed his eyes. Moments later, he startled awake to the sound of a chime. He rose and didn't bother to pull on pants. If it was the fuck, he wouldn't need them.

He slapped his hand to the panel, and the door slid back.

Varik startled and took a huge step back, grabbing the towel as it slipped. "Corvus?"

"It's *Master* to you."

Two goons each grabbed an arm and marched Varik away from his small, dusty sanctuary.

Cifer cradled the lined box and led the crew of *The Treasure* down the ramp. The Hiargus spaceport was spectacular. The main building was iridescent glass that jutted several stories into the soft blue sky. A gathering of willowy-robed beings waited a notable distance from *The Treasure*. The contrast of their appearance to the crew, in their coveralls and boots, wasn't lost on Cifer. They were royalty, and he and his team were the hired help.

Resigned to a long walk, he tucked the box under one arm and took Blaize's hand in his. Dez and Cyra were to his right, and Veda, Rhysa, and Bodi followed. As soon as they cleared the ramp, the royals moved toward them until they met halfway. That was unexpected.

The king dipped his head in acknowledgement, his gaze never leaving Cifer.

"I retrieved what you wanted."

"We have transferred the remaining credits due you." The king's voice was clear, like the glass of the building, with equally sharp edges.

Cifer released Blaize's hand, retrieved his data pad, and tapped his access codes with one hand, confirming the deposit had been made to his working account. The balance, which had once been zero, contained a significant number of zeroes after the transfer. He couldn't help but smile as he handed over the box. The king passed it to the man on his left, who promptly opened the container. A faint glow emanated, tinging the male's face slightly pink. Nothing like the glow that had been filling the corridors before Cifer had asked Veda to lock it away.

"And the man who took it?" the king asked.

Cifer dropped his gaze. "I'm sorry."

The king nodded, a slight movement, confirming he understood what Cifer didn't want to say out loud. An older female in the back sniffed, her hand went to her chest, and a male who might be her husband draped his arm around her and clutched her close. The celebratory rush faded slightly in the presence of parents who'd lost their child. Their love didn't fade because their child was an adult, probably a thief, and certainly a maker of poor decisions.

Cifer's heart grew heavy as he considered how his own experience of bad decisions had led to him being in the wrong place at the wrong time. Kidnapped instead of running away, but maybe his parents didn't know that part. He didn't know if they were still alive, not that he'd ever have a chance to explain if they were.

Blaize slipped her hand into his and leaned into his shoulder. He drew her strength into him and stood a little taller.

"We are grateful to have the Heart's Fire stone returned." The young male who held the box stepped forward. "My betrothed and I can complete the rituals, and our pairing will be blessed by the gods."

Cifer wasn't sure how a glowing stone could help make a relationship work, but good for them.

"We hope you can stay for the wedding," the king said.

"We have rooms prepared in the palace. Your crew is welcome to join you."

Rhysa burst forward and addressed the male to the king's right. "Absolutely. I love weddings."

The king raised his hand above his head, and a clear aircraft, built with the same iridescent glass as the building, landed a short distance away, barely disturbing the air.

Blaize squeezed his fingers and gasped. "That is so cool. I have to find out how that works."

Cifer looked at Dez. He, in turn, focused on Captain Cyra.

"Thank you for your hospitality. We'd love to stay for a short visit."

Cifer noted the captain's emphasis on "short," which was smart. He had no idea how long the marital ceremonial processes took on Hiargus.

The king's ship held all of them comfortably, and after a brief flight, they landed on a balcony of what must be the palace.

For the first time, Cifer noted that the glass, which also made up most of the huge building, was opaque. He'd had a clear view of the buildings, homes, and landscape, flying over. Interesting material. Cifer considered the value to other planets. His calculations increased as soon as he entered the building and found it cool but well-lit. In a glass building, it should have been on the far side of uncomfortable. It would have been, with regular glass. Cifer held back his burning questions, but there was potential for trade there. He could practically smell it.

A beautiful young female emerged from a hallway, flanked by an older couple, a male, and two younger females. She crossed the room directly to the male holding the box with the orb. He lifted the metal lid, and she reached inside, cradling the sphere in her hands. The male put the box down. The rest of the Hiargus natives shifted into a circle around the couple. Cifer and Blaize, along with the crew of *The Treasure*, completed the ring. The orb glowed softly at first. Then, the male placed his hands over hers.

Fiery light filled the room. No longer pink, it was nearly red with yellow sparks.

The light seemed to infuse Cifer's skin with warmth, traveling through his arm to where he still held Blaize's hand. He glanced at his lover. Her gaze locked on his. Her heartbeat pulsed through his veins. The love filling his heart seemed to burst and flood every cell of his being. A murmur of words surrounded them. Cifer shifted and took Blaize's other hand in his. One thought echoed through him, escaped from between his lips. "I'm yours, always."

Blaize said the same words at the same time.

As if a key had turned in a lock.

Clapping brought Cifer back to the room. He released one of Blaize's hands reluctantly and faced the group. The orb was back to being the glass ball Cifer had found on Kolben. The couple handed the gem back to the king.

"Congratulations," the king said to the couple before he turned to Cifer and Blaize. "I did warn you not to touch it too much."

Cifer clacked his jaw. "That thing"—Cifer pointed at the sphere—"has nothing to do with the love I feel for Blaize."

"Correct," the king said. "It merely recognizes what the stars have put in motion and...solidifies it."

Blaize clutched Cifer's arm to his body. "Good."

"Now we celebrate."

The smiling couple led the way to a banquet room filled with people. Bodi hesitated at the doorway.

"What's wrong?" Blaize dropped Cifer's hand to take

Bodi's shoulders. Her wings were fluttering, and beads of sweat had appeared on her forehead.

"I have to go back to the ship. You go ahead. I'll be fine."

Cifer wrinkled his brow. "The transporter, or *The Treasure*?"

"I have to get out of here. I should have stayed on our ship."

The others had emptied the chamber. Cifer led Bodi to one of the benches that flanked the perimeter. "Sit. Breathe."

Blaize sat beside Bodi, drawing her down. "What is going on? You've been nervous since we found Cifer on the ship. What are you worried about, Bodi? What are you hiding?"

Bodi slid her hand into a pocket of her coveralls, retrieving her data pad. She tapped a few times and handed it to Blaize.

Blaize read, scrolled, and read some more. This continued long enough that Cifer shifted on his feet. Blaize's face took on the same expression as when the engine was doing something she didn't like.

"Oh shit." Blaize looked up from the data pad. "Why didn't you say anything?"

Bodi winced. "At first, I thought my mother was trying to manipulate me. Then I thought it would blow over when we were on the long legs of the journey to Kolben and back to Cassan. Since no one tried anything on Cassan, I figured it was a joke. One of my sisters stirring the pot, maybe." Bodi's wings fluttered so fast they blurred, and a buzzing sound filled the cavernous room.

"But they think we've kidnapped you." Blaize stood and took a position in front of Cifer. "They think Cifer was sent to kill you, and you didn't disabuse them of that notion." Blaize stomped her foot. "How could you?"

"It's not him they're accusing. In fact, I've told them we have extra protection. There have been calls too." Bodi dropped her head into her hands. "I'm not ready for this."

"Ready for what?" Blaize asked.

Bodi held out her hand, and Blaize responded by giving her back the data pad. Bodi tapped and swiped a few more times before thrusting it back into Blaize's hands.

Cifer peered over Blaize's shoulder. An image of six males of varying shapes and sizes, all well-built and arguably handsome, wearing uniforms draped in medals and other accessories, filled the screen. "Who are they?"

Bodi grimaced. "My...um...royal guard."

"Your family's mad because you left without your security detail? That doesn't seem like that big a deal." Cifer wasn't sure about a normal family's reaction, but Bodi's fear seemed exaggerated.

Bodi shook her head. "My royal guard are my future hive. My...mates?"

"Oh." Blaize gave Cifer a wide-eyed glance. "And they think we kidnapped you because you didn't take them when you left the planet with us to be the communications officer."

Bodi nodded, her wings slowing to a flutter. "And if I don't agree to meet them on Cassan, they're coming after me."

First, last, and always, thank you to my husband for supporting my writing in every way. I love you!

Special nod to my friend and fellow author, Ryan T. Osborn, for his book title which inspired Varik's ship name.

Thank you to the Red Reines for everything you do.

Thank you to Brandi Doane McCann for another amazing cover.

Thank you to Dayna Hart for digging into the chaos bucket of a draft and helping me craft a story that worked.

Thank you to my amazing beta readers who made this book infinitely better.

Thank you to Jenny Rardon for sorting out the commas and other mechanical issues, and generally being a rockstar!

Thank you to Passionate Ink for providing a safe and educational forum for erotic authors, especially my morning sprint partners whose ongoing support is priceless.

And, most importantly, thank you to my readers who make it worth all the struggles to write!

Award-winning, best-selling author, Jordyn Kross, is an unapologetically naughty novelist who spent years honing her writing skills with tech manuals and marginal poetry before finding her passion for writing sexy, boundary-stretching happily-ever-afters.

When she's not writing, she's attempting to garden in the desert Southwest, hiking with her insane pound posse, and admiring that handsome man wandering around her house who continues to stay.

Jordyn enjoys saucy double entendres, pretending to be an extrovert, and is well-known for having no filter. And when she's not in social media jail, she can be found on Facebook, Instagram, and BookBub, or hiding in a dark cave peering out at the X file formerly knows as Twitter.

www.ingramcontent.com/pod-product-compliance
Lightning Source LLC
Chambersburg PA
CBHW061244310726
48971CB00007B/2205